SHADOWS & VEILS

EDITED BY IAN SKEWIS

First published in Scotland in 2025 by Brae Books

All characters in this publication are fictitious and any resemblance to real persons, living or dead, is purely coincidental.

www.braebooks.com

Book cover design © Ian Skewis 2025

Mysterious scene with house in forest (royalty-free image) uploaded via Freepik

Print ISBN: 978-1-9193234-0-4

CONTENTS

SHADOWS & VEILS

TALES OF THE SUPERNATURAL

PREFACE

When I was first asked to assemble this book I was very excited but I had no real idea of where it would lead – I have Jeannette Ellwood and Sue Mowforth to thank for that.

I had previously worked with these lovely authors on their travel book, *Nuns, Guns & Disappearing Suns*. They wanted their book edited and proofread and as it contained photographs they wanted them edited too. Editing photos for a book was a first for me and I approached it with some degree of nervousness but the end result was a good one for all concerned and it was another skill I added to my editing services.

My intrepid travel writers, however, asked me to embark on another journey that would take me into even more far-reaching territory. Would I assemble an anthology for their book group?

Of course, said I, and I soon got down to business.

The first thing I did was to expand the initial competition to encompass authors beyond the original book group, which I think has made for an even richer anthology. I then read through all the short stories that were submitted and chose the winning entries. Then I edited and proofread them. I also designed the book cover and took charge of publishing duties as well. In effect, I have become a publisher.

However, it struck me that given that all the authors were providing their stories for free because this book is for charity, then I should do the same, despite my much bigger workload. I waived my fees and I have assembled this book free of charge. The pay-off, if you will, is my newly acquired set of skills as a publisher, typesetter and book designer and it also sees the launch of my wee publishing house, Brae Books.

I am really proud of the work everyone has done on this anthology and I must thank Jeannette and Sue for devising this wonderful project.

All the royalties from this book are going to the PD James Memorial Fund which helps provide modest long-term pensions to writers at the end of their careers.

Thank you for purchasing our little book and for helping those in need.

Best Wishes,
Ian Skewis, 2025.

https://www.societyofauthors.org/Grants/P-D-James-Memorial-Fund

1

THE LONGING

JEANNETTE ELLWOOD

'I can't believe it. There's that piano again.' She stopped the hoover and rushed into the music room. The piano lid stood open, but all was quiet.

'I'm sure I heard it,' she muttered to herself.

She had been so happy to find this enchanting house. It suited her beautifully, set in the middle of a neat garden, with the promise of a pretty climbing rose draping over the front porch ready to bloom in the summer. The views over the fields to the dreaming hills gave her a sense of belonging, of coming home.

At last, she'd found her refuge – it had taken so long.

The village seemed friendly enough too, though no one had actually spoken to her yet. *Can't think why*, she mused one day, as she wandered down the long winding lane to the pond – one of her favourite places. Someone had thoughtfully positioned a bench there so people could feed the ducks that busily explored the forest of reeds at the water's edge. She sat and watched with interest as a small group of children with nets and buckets tried to catch the elusive tadpoles gathered in clumps under the lily pads. Her gaze lingered on a little girl, a finger in her mouth, watching wistfully.

A rush of sympathy and longing swept over her. She stood up suddenly – thrusting those uncomfortable feelings to the back of her mind.

Waving gaily at the children, she picked up her basket of groceries, preparing for the walk home. They all ignored her, as children do, intent on their task.

Although I come here every day, no one seems to want to speak to me, she thought. *I still feel like a stranger, unknown, unnoticed*. She blinked back sudden tears, telling herself, *Maybe it's me. Maybe I'm not friendly enough. Maybe I don't smile enough.*

As she arrived at the big double gates leading to her drive, she was surprised to see that the plant pots, which had once lined the path, were now flanking the front door. Filled with daffodils, they looked very pretty, but *she* hadn't put them there. Her annoyance flared – was someone playing tricks on her? This was beyond anything! She opened the heavy door and walked straight through to the kitchen, putting her shopping on the table. Unbelievably, the oven was on and the seductive smell of a baking cake filled her nostrils. What *was* going on?

She stomped angrily upstairs to check the bedrooms and the bathroom. No one. As she came downstairs, she made for the umbrella stand by the front door, grabbed a walking stick (just in case) and cautiously peered into the music room. Again, no one. The only other room was what she called the library – filled with books, a comfortable settee, a TV, and a couple of armchairs. Still, no one. But this time, she sensed something – a strange presence, as though someone had just left the room.

Slightly shaken, she went to the pantry and grabbed a box of jam tarts – her comfort food. Putting the kettle on the hob, ready to make herself a cup of tea, she sat down, suddenly sensing the house had changed. She looked around the familiar cosiness of her kitchen, but it no longer felt like hers. The electric oven and dishwasher sat quietly in the corners, strange and out of place, like uninvited guests in a home she thought she knew. 'Don't be silly,' she muttered to herself. 'I'm just tired – not sleeping well. Too many things on my mind.' She shook off the strange feeling of disorientation.

As she sat there, the memory of her dream from the night before flooded back. The feeling of acute loss returned, sharp and unshakable. She strained to recall what it was she needed to find, but for the life of her, it wouldn't come.

I feel really weird, she thought, a sense of confusion creeping in. *I can't seem to keep up with what appears to be happening here.*

Getting up from her seat, she changed into her boots and wandered into the garden, looking for some kind of refuge or at least reassurance. As she stepped out, its once familiar paths, plants, and shadows seemed to shimmer and change, as though the very fabric of the place was shifting before her eyes. She put her hand out to the rough stone wall for support as the air around her seemed to rearrange itself. A sudden wave of joy and fulfilment washed over her. She inhaled deeply, an intoxicating scent of honeysuckle filled her senses, and for a moment she could hear a nightingale singing sweetly from the high branches of the sycamore tree. She lifted her face to the sky, basking in the warmth of the afternoon sun.

'I just love being here,' she whispered, overwhelmed by an unexplainable sense of delight. But as quickly as it had come, the uncanny vista slipped away. She hesitantly walked down the now rain-drenched path, automatically bending to pluck a rogue weed or two, intending to toss them into the gardener's wheelbarrow. Splashing through a puddle she became aware of the weight of her soggy jacket dragging heavily on her shoulders.

She lifted her eyes to the sky, hoping to hear the silvery notes of the nightingale, but there was only silence. All she could see were heavy clouds a brooding shade of grey, as the air grew thick with the smell of damp earth. What had made her think it was a good gardening day? What in heaven had made her think she had a gardener for that matter?

Hurrying back into the house, she draped her jacket over the radiator in the kitchen, grateful for its warmth. Leaving her boots by the back door, she moved quickly into the library, eager for the comforting fire she expected to find there.

I'll read that novel by Jane Austen – so true to life, she thought, smiling to herself as she sank into her favourite armchair, instinctively reaching for the book she'd left on the side table. But it wasn't there.

Confused, she turned her head, only to find the table was now laden with a tray and two glasses of wine.

She leapt to her feet in shock. Her eyes darted to the bookshelf – there it was, the book, sitting untouched, just as it had always been. She shivered suddenly, a coldness creeping over her. She stretched her hands toward the fire – but there was only a couple of blackened logs and powdery grey ash. No flames, no warmth, no fire.

'What's happening to me?' she murmured. 'Am I imagining things? Could I be dreaming?'

The house again felt insubstantial and unwelcoming. Her heart raced, and she backed out of the library, her eyes scanning the dim room, half expecting someone to slip past her. Her thoughts spun wildly. Stumbling into the hallway, she grasped her stick once more, its solid weight offering comfort to her trembling hands. 'What's happening to me?' she pleaded to the heavy silence. She closed her eyes and took a few deep breaths, trying to steady herself, her voice trembling. *Maybe I should find somewhere else to stay, away from lingering half-memories and dreams...* Wearily, she turned to climb the stairs, hoping the cool calm of her bedroom would ease her restless spirit.

As she reached the top step, her eyes were drawn to a half-open door leading to a room tucked under the eaves. Still holding the stick, she crept toward it, her feet making no sound on the thick carpet. Pushing the door further open, she was astonished by what she saw: a toy-strewn, sunlit room, with a soft pink blanket draped over a rocking chair, a cot in the corner, and pretty lace curtains fluttering slightly in a warm, gentle breeze. The faint scent of lavender polish lingered in the air, mingling with the sweet, powdery smell of baby talc. The nursery looked just as it had been so long ago. Creeping in, stick still in hand, her fingers brushed against the worn, soft edge of a faded cushion, its pattern a blur of colours dimmed by the passage of time. Hearing a faint sound behind her, she turned. There in the doorway stood a slim, pretty woman with dark hair, cradling a baby and holding the hand of a little girl.

The woman looked straight at her, searchingly, as if seeing right through her. She eventually smiled and said, 'At last,' her voice echoing strangely as though from a distant land. 'I've been hoping we might meet. I've seen you several times in my kitchen and once in the library. Richard, my husband, has felt your presence in the house, especially in our music room. We think you've heard him play.' She paused, her gaze softening. 'My name is Alicia. What's yours?'

Taking her time, she slowly replied, 'Alice... I think. I can't quite remember.' Dropping the walking stick to the floor, she took a step toward the little girl whose wide brown eyes stared curiously at the lady who had bent over her cot so many times. A familiar rush of emptiness swept over Alice as she opened her arms, hoping the little one would fill them. But the child only clung closer to her mother's skirts.

'No,' said the young woman, 'she is not for you.' She gestured gently toward the door. 'I think you should go downstairs into our garden, I am almost sure it's there you will find what you've been looking for.'

With a final glance around the nursery, Alice took a steadying breath, and moved silently past the little family, toward the stairs. The young woman watched her with a warm smile, moving aside to allow her to pass.

She walked slowly down, her heart growing lighter with each step, as if a weight she had carried for years was silently lifting. The air felt fresher somehow, the colours brighter, and as she stepped outside, she found herself in her old garden where the scent of honeysuckle drifted through the air, the sound of birdsong filling the skies. There, by the roses that climbed up the front porch, stood the little girl she had longed for, her golden curls catching the sunlight, her face radiant with a smile. The child looked up at her, her eyes wide with recognition and joy, and without a word, she reached out her little arms. Her mother knelt, gathering her into a warm embrace, feeling the small heartbeat against her own, that precious, long-missed presence that made her feel whole once more. She held her close, breathing in her somehow familiar sweet smell.

She became aware of Alicia and her children standing in the doorway behind her. Turning slightly, she smiled and gave a slight wave of thanks for the guidance she felt she'd been given. Walking down the path with the little girl's hand in her own, she felt as if she was floating. This small hand was familiar in a way she couldn't explain, as if it belonged to a piece of herself she hadn't known she'd lost.

The child looked up at her with eyes the same shade of gentle turquoise as her own, her hair the colour of sunlit honey – just as she'd always imagined her baby might look. She realised then that this little girl was more than a memory or a dream; she was a part of herself, a piece of her heart she had carried quietly all her life. She squeezed the child's hand and felt the warmth of that gentle connection, a wordless love that filled the empty places she had never allowed herself to acknowledge.

They reached the edge of the garden, where the flowers grew wild and fragrant, weaving their colours together under the dappled sunlight. She knelt down beside her daughter, brushing a stray lock of hair from her face, and felt a bittersweet joy in the simplicity of that gesture, in finally being here, in this place, together. The garden seemed to hum with life, the air filled with birdsong and the gentle rustling of leaves, as if nature itself embraced this moment.

In that space, she felt the memories of all her loves and all her losses settle into the dim, almost forgotten past. She knew then that she had carried the joy of this child she'd never had in life, like a treasured keepsake that had made her who she was. And as they stood close together at the garden's edge, she whispered to the little girl, 'I have loved you always,' and knew that, somehow, it was enough.

They lingered there, in the garden, sunlight casting soft shadows around them, surrounded by the quiet beauty of the flowers and trees. Then they continued down the path together, taking their time, savouring each step, because there was no rush, no fear of parting, no need to look back.

Behind them, the young woman watched from the doorway, her gaze filled with quiet, loving understanding. Richard had once shown her an old photograph of his Great Aunt Alice, the woman with golden hair who had always loved this garden and had died there mourning her stillborn only child. Alicia turned to look at him standing behind her, a gentle smile forming. 'I think she's found what she was looking for,' she whispered, watching the figures disappear around the bend in the path. She closed the door quietly, returning to her family and a house finally at peace.

Alice and her daughter lingered among the flowers, the child picking quantities of daisies, clutching them in her tiny hand, saving them for daisy chains, happy and safe in the quiet garden. And then, with unhurried steps, they melted into the green haze of the nearby meadow, smiling fondly at each other, hands still held fast.

2

THE ESSENCE OF BROUGHTON HOUSE

CHAUNTELLE WRIGHT

A dark stain bloomed across the ceiling of Broughton House's foyer, a perfect rosette of water damage that Caroline Avery hadn't noticed during their viewing. Yet now, as she inhaled her first breath as the mansion's new owner, the stain seemed to pulse slightly, like something breathing behind the plaster. The air carried a cloying sweetness that coated her tongue and crept down her throat, almost suffocating in its intensity.

'What is that smell?' she whispered, more to herself than to her husband.

James set down their suitcases, his eyes following the grand staircase that curved upward like a spine. 'Just old-house must,' he replied. 'Nothing a good airing won't fix. This is it. We are now the owners of a mansion!'

Caroline smiled and nodded absently, watching how the autumn light through the leaded windows cast latticed shadows across the entryway floor, like prison bars, she thought, then immediately chided herself for the morbid comparison. They'd bought the Georgian mansion at an absurdly low price, a perfect empty-nest reward after decades of child-rearing and career sacrifices. A perfect early-retirement project.

The estate agent's words echoed in her mind: *The previous owner was quite... motivated to sell. It's been empty for years.* The woman had touched her crucifix pendant when she'd said it, her smile never reaching her eyes.

As they explored the house, Caroline felt the sweet smell intensify in certain rooms. It became almost unbearable in the room chosen to become her study. It was a small but lovely room at the end of the upstairs hallway with a large bay window overlooking the tangled gardens. When she mentioned the scent again, James merely shrugged. 'I don't smell anything unusual, love. Perhaps it's just the flowers the agent left?'

But the bouquet in the foyer held only dry, odourless roses with petals that crumbled at the slightest touch.

That night, Caroline dreamed of women with hollow eyes watching her from the corners of rooms, their translucent forms wavering like reflections in disturbed water. They whispered a single phrase in unison: 'She has chosen you.' She awoke drenched in sweat, the sheets twisted around her legs like binding ropes, that sickly-sweet scent so strong she gagged.

In the bathroom mirror, bizarrely her reflection seemed... delayed. When she raised her hand to touch her face, the mirrored Caroline hesitated for a heartbeat before mimicking the gesture. She frowned and shook her head at her own silliness. Just a trick of the light, she told herself. Just new-house nerves.

As days passed, Caroline found herself drawn repeatedly to her study, but she sat there, abandoning her half-finished novel, to stare at the faded wallpaper, running her fingers over a section that felt different – cooler, almost vibrating beneath her touch. The smell was overpowering there, bringing with it intense headaches that drilled behind her eyes and yet... a strange euphoria.

James noticed the changes in her. 'You seem distracted,' he said over dinner one night, untouched food growing cold between them. 'And your eyes, they look different somehow.'

'Different?' Caroline asked, her voice distant.

'Darker. Almost... not yours.'

She laughed it off, but later examined herself in the mirror. Her normally hazel eyes had deepened to an unnatural obsidian. When she blinked, she could swear she saw another woman's face superimposed over her own for a fraction of a second – older, with aristocratic features and a knowing smile.

The next morning, Caroline found a small bruise on her wrist – perfectly circular, like a fingerprint. By evening, another had appeared on her shoulder, then her collarbone. James didn't notice; he assured her he couldn't see them. But she felt them – burning cold, as if marked by unseen hands.

A week after moving in, Caroline discovered an old photograph tucked inside a book in the library, a formal portrait of a Victorian family in front of Broughton House. The patriarch stood stern and proud, but his wife's face was blurred, as if she'd moved during the exposure. Something about her outline seemed familiar.

The whispers started three days later. At first, just indistinct murmuring that could have been the house settling or wind in the eaves. Then phrases, clear as crystal, spoken directly behind her when she sat alone in her study:

'Find us.'

'Open the wall.'

'We've waited so long.'

During a particularly sleepless night, Caroline found herself in her study without remembering how she'd even got there. The room was bathed in moonlight that seemed to concentrate on one wall panel. Without conscious thought, her fingers traced an invisible seam. Something clicked beneath her touch.

A door swung inward, revealing a narrow spiral staircase ascending into darkness. The sweet smell erupted from the opening like a physical force, nearly knocking her backward. Caroline's hand found the wall to steady herself, leaving a perfect, bloody handprint, though she had no wounds.

'Caroline?' James called from down the hallway. 'Who are you talking to?'

She closed the hidden door hastily, heart hammering. 'No one,' she called back. 'Just... working through some dialogue for my book.'

But later, when James slept, Caroline returned. This time she brought a torch, its beam cutting weakly through the thick darkness of the stairwell. As she ascended, the wooden steps groaned beneath her weight – not the normal settling of old wood, but pained, human-like moans.

At the top, another door awaited, slightly ajar. The circular room beyond contained nothing but a pedestal in its centre, upon which rested an ornate perfume bottle of deep-purple glass. The bottle's surface was carved with tiny female faces, their expressions shifting between ecstasy and agony when the light touched them.

Inside, a liquid shimmered with its own inner luminescence, moving against gravity, climbing the glass walls as if reaching for her. She heard a humming sound. It wasn't coming from the bottle, Caroline realised, but from the walls themselves – from the house, vibrating at a frequency that resonated in her bones.

Without conscious decision, her hand reached for the bottle. The glass burned cold against her skin, yet she couldn't release it. The stopper came free with a sound like a distant scream.

The scent exploded around her, no longer just sweet but complex and ancient; myrrh and decay, honey and blood, desire and despair. Caroline's vision kaleidoscoped, reality splintering into overlapping images: the room as it was now; the room filled with women in clothing from different eras, all watching her with identical black eyes; the room as a dark void where something ancient and hungry pulsed.

She brought the bottle to her nose, then her lips – not to drink, but almost as if it demanded to be kissed. A single drop touched her tongue, and Caroline felt herself fragmenting, her consciousness stretching like melted toffee, extending into every corner of Broughton House, feeling its foundations, its history, its hunger.

When she returned to her body, dawn was breaking. The bottle was stoppered and back on its pedestal. Caroline descended the stairs on trembling legs, closed the hidden door, and returned to bed beside her sleeping husband. Later, in the bathroom mirror, her reflection smiled before she did. She definitely wasn't imagining this, she thought.

The transformation accelerated. Her skin grew luminous, wrinkles smoothing away overnight. Silver strands in her hair darkened back to rich auburn. James marvelled at her renewed vitality, never noticing how her shadow sometimes moved independently of her body, or how mirrors captured multiple reflections when she passed.

Caroline visited the hidden room nightly now, applying the perfume to her pulse points like an addict. Each application bound her more tightly to Broughton House, threading her essence into its structure. Sometimes she found herself standing in empty rooms with no memory of how she'd got there, one hand pressed against a wall as if listening to the building's heartbeat.

Her writing changed. Pages filled with the same phrase repeated endlessly: *We are Broughton House.* When James discovered these pages and confronted her, Caroline had no memory of writing them. That night, for the first time, she felt afraid of what was happening.

'I need to leave,' she whispered to her reflection. In the mirror, her face shifted between her own and dozens of others, all shaking their heads in unison.

'We cannot leave,' their voices chorused in her mind. 'We are home now.'

Caroline packed a suitcase while James slept. At the front door, her legs simply stopped working. Her hand couldn't grasp the doorknob. The house wouldn't release her.

Desperate, she woke James, words tumbling out about the hidden room, the bottle, the women trapped inside Broughton House. He held her, concerned, then led her back to bed, promising to investigate in the morning, clearly believing she was suffering delusions.

But morning revealed James standing transfixed in her study, the hidden jib door hanging open, the sweet scent filling the room. 'I found it,' he whispered, his voice strangely flat. 'I found what was changing you.'

Caroline watched in horror as he ascended the stairs, calling his name as she followed. In the circular room, James held the purple bottle, examining it with clinical detachment.

'James, don't...'

'They told me everything,' he interrupted, his eyes reflecting the bottle's strange inner light. 'How you'll leave me otherwise. How you'll age and die. But this...' he held up the bottle, '...this keeps you with me forever.'

'Who told you?' Caroline whispered, though she already knew.

James's smile wasn't his own. 'Broughton House did.'

Before she could stop him, he removed the stopper and drank deeply. His body convulsed, the bottle slipping from his grasp to shatter on the floor. The liquid seeped into the floorboards, which absorbed it greedily as James collapsed.

Caroline knelt beside him, cradling his head as his eyes turned black, then vacant. His skin grew translucent, then began to literally fade. As his form dissipated in her arms, his voice echoed from everywhere and nowhere:

'I've made the sacrifice they asked for. A male essence, given willingly. You're free now, Caroline. But I'll be here, in the walls, waiting for you to return.'

By nightfall, no trace of James remained. The police found no evidence of foul play, only a distraught widow insisting her husband had vanished before her eyes. They discovered no hidden room, no broken bottle; the house had sealed its secrets away.

Caroline fled Broughton House the next day, the sweet smell following her, though fainter with distance. For years, she moved from place to place, never staying long enough to form attachments. But as she aged, rapidly now, the years stolen back with interest, she felt the pull growing stronger.

On her deathbed in a sterile hospital room, Caroline smelt it again, that sweet, cloying scent. Opening her eyes, she saw not doctors or nurses, but the circular room at Broughton House. James stood waiting, eternally young, surrounded by the women with black eyes.

'Welcome home,' they said in unison.

FIFTEEN YEARS LATER, a young family toured Broughton House; a couple with twin daughters. As they entered the study, one girl froze, her head tilting as if listening.

'What's that smell?' she asked, her eyes fixed on the wall where no door was visible.

Her twin inhaled deeply, a strange smile spreading across her face. 'The lady in the wall says it's for us,' she whispered. 'She says we'll never have to be apart. Not ever.'

Their mother laughed nervously, tugging them toward the door. 'There's no lady in the wall, girls.'

But as they left, both girls looked back in perfect unison, their eyes reflecting something ancient and patient.

Broughton House had chosen again.

3

THE SHADOW DEBT

CAMPBELL CHRISTIE

'Night, night.'

'Night.'

'Sweet dreams.'

'Sweet dreams.'

'See you in the morning.'

'See you in the morning.'

'Love you…'

There was a long pause. Alan lay in bed with his back to Sarah, waiting for a response.

'Do we have to do this every night?' she said with a sigh.

'What do you mean?'

'This routine, do we have to do it every night?'

'Well… it helps.'

'How?'

'I can't sleep. Sometimes, when we argue and don't say it, I don't sleep.'

'I know, but can't we just say goodnight? Can't that be enough?'

'I thought it was cute, like a thing that just me and you do.'

'We don't have to do it all the time.'

'But it's our routine.'

'I know, exactly. It's a routine, and sometimes I'm tired and can't be bothered. Saying "I love you" out of habit doesn't really count. You should say it when you mean it.'

'But I always mean it.'

Another long pause.

'Anyway, I'm knackered, Alan. Goodnight.'

'I love you.'

'Night.'

Alan resigned himself to rubbing his feet against hers and along her leg. He knew she liked it, and the repetitive motion helped him relax. They were both tired from the daily grind of middle-aged parenthood, their days revolving around routines and compromises that left no time to savour their lives together, leaving only vague memories.

He turned onto his preferred sleeping side, facing the window. Sleep came before he was aware of it. Sometimes he would be lying waiting for it, and this would always be counter-productive, but tonight he had drifted into that transitional phase between wakefulness and sleep. His mind filled with fractured images that led him into a slumber dream of walking along a dark street, past familiar faces of people he had never met, phantom memories of motion. He walked the edge of the kerb and slipped off into a hypnic jerk that immediately startled him awake, heart racing from adrenaline.

He sat up and looked around, hoping he hadn't disturbed Sarah. Was that a heart attack? He was in the danger zone: stress, a bad diet, and family history all forged a potential sword of Damocles ready to strike him down.

The curtains breathed in the darkness, even though the window wasn't open. The shape within them wasn't just shadows; it was a defined form, gaunt and cloaked, with an unnerving stillness that radiated a chill that raised goosebumps. The shadow in the curtains looked like death itself, the silent spectre pulled from ancient myths. Sarah's breathing beside him was a fragile counterpoint to the dread that filled his head.

This wasn't the first time. Terror had seized him in the night before; even as a boy, he had felt this dread, but it had always been intangible. He had seen a shadowy figure inhabiting the curtains before, and every time, he convinced himself it was just shadows. Until recently. The shadow had been growing, slowly forming night by night into something undeniably dark and sinister. He could make out the hood, the long arms, the flowing, slender body.

Don't be daft, man, he admonished himself.

The cold sweat and rapid heartbeat were convincing him

there was a threat, but his rational mind persevered. *No, it isn't; it's just shadows in the folds of the curtains.* He stared and stared at them until reasoning settled his mind.

He checked his phone: 10:22. He lay back down and closed his eyes, imagining climbing out of the window, floating above the rooftops, escaping. Soon he was fast asleep.

12:02. Alan shot up again, eyes wide open. The shadow from the curtains was upon him, skeletal fingers emanating from its sleeve, gripping his throat. A contorted darkness seemed to peer from the hood, leeching the life and soul from him as he sat rigid. This time reasoning wouldn't prevail. It wasn't just shadows in the curtains. Something had him in its grasp, its malevolence bringing death upon him.

His heart hammered frantically. A final surge of strength broke his paralysis, and he flung his arm out, knocking over the bedside lamp with a crash.

Sarah woke with shock. She screamed, then shouted at him, 'What the hell are you doing, you idiot?!'

Alan clutched his chest, unable to breathe, yet free from the grasp of death.

Sarah switched on the main light, checking the damage to the lamp rather than her husband. 'You broke the bloody lamp! That was a wedding gift!'

Alan still couldn't catch his breath. He stood up and grabbed the curtains, his legs barely able to hold him up. Finally, air filled his lungs. He sat back down, exhausted and horrified.

Sarah continued inspecting the broken lamp. 'Honestly, Alan, what is wrong with you? Look at what you've done. You scared the life out of me. You could have hurt me.'

Her anger flickered to fear as she saw his vacant, pallid face, beaded with perspiration. She touched his arm. His pupils had dilated, and his face began to contort as if he were going to cry, but he held back when he saw her unforgiving look.

'Maybe you should sleep in the spare room.'

'What?' His mind wasn't fully present; the fear still lingered.

Sarah went to the en suite, venting her anger through half-formed words he couldn't make out. Alan gathered his pillow and spare bedding and left. Passing their daughter's room, he checked on her – fast asleep, unharmed, oblivious. She was his reason for enduring the daily grind, his miracle who wasn't supposed to survive her premature birth at twenty-nine weeks. He always worried there was a price to pay for her existence.

The spare room had Venetian blinds, not curtains. No chance of the curtain ghoul here. But sleep wouldn't come. The bed felt wrong – too firm, too narrow, lacking the familiar groove beside Sarah. He'd always had problems sleeping until he met her; her presence gave him the comfort he needed. Although, that was the only comfort left in their marriage. Their relationship was fractured beyond repair; two people growing in different directions, their wants and needs misaligned. Sarah demanded more from him than anyone ever had, wielding her disappointment like a weapon during fights, each word designed to wound, to remind him how he never measured up.

Did they actually love each other? He'd always thought so, deep down, but nothing remained certain. Their relationship existed in contradictions: they functioned well and terribly, loved and hated, understood and misunderstood each other in equal measure. How did two people once so in love end up in such darkness? Was the darkness of their relationship conjuring these terrifying apparitions? If so, his marriage was truly beyond saving.

By morning, exhausted, he slipped back into the old routine, putting to one side the night's horrors and thoughts of leaving.

Troubled by the shadowy visits, Alan researched sleep disorders and even paranormal phenomena. The Greeks had given death a name, Thanatos, and given it form. Was that what he saw? Every culture had names for things waiting in darkness: Draugr, Pisadeira, Mare, Old Hag. He felt haunted, even though he had never believed in ghosts or the supernatural.

A romantic text message he copied and pasted from the internet tentatively reconciled them, and the next night he was back in their bed. They avoided the bedtime routine, both too weary for conflict. So many times, a passing comment had escalated into an argument, leaving them both too stressed to sleep. Tonight, they were wiser. Sarah rubbed his legs with her feet, and with the comfort of her beside him, he fell asleep quickly.

Alan was deep in REM when the shadows began to move. The streetlights outside went out all at once. Darkness swelled through the bedroom as his breathing turned heavy and erratic. His eyes snapped open to absolute darkness. He couldn't move, trapped in sleep paralysis. He tried to call out, but his breath was sucked from his lungs with each attempt.

Then the darkness thickened, revealing the hooded figure, now more solid, more present, looming over him, its cloak enveloping him like a shroud. Through paralysed eyes, he watched it reach out. His heart fluttered so violently he thought it would stop. The form manifested within the darkness, something his mind refused to comprehend. Its features shifted, revealing glimpses of malevolence that shouldn't exist. Pure terror overcame him as cold sweat drenched his skin. The entity's presence crept through his nervous system like an electrical current. He was alive yet dying, awake yet dormant, utterly alone with something that had studied human fear since time began.

Then the shadow moved toward Sarah, pressing down on her with suffocating weight. She stirred with a soft moan. His survival instincts surged through the paralysis, breaking it with a force of will so great that the shadow lost control of him. He lunged forward, beating at the figure with his fists as hard as he could. He screamed as he fought the shadow off. Then it retaliated, and his breath was choked away until he collapsed into darkness.

Morning light woke him. His first thought was of the vivid night terror; he felt like he had died in his sleep. He looked over at Sarah. Her dead eyes stared back. Her blue lips were swollen, and blood oozed from her mouth and caked her battered face. A broken tooth lay next to her on the pillow.

Alan jumped out of the bed. Looking at his bloodied hands, he backed out of the room, away from his wife, and into the next room to instinctively check on his daughter.

She was unharmed, fast asleep.

Returning to the bedroom, he saw Sarah's body in an unnatural position, contorted as if from a struggle. He reached over to touch her leg – it was cold. At this point, he didn't know what had happened or what he should do. On autopilot, he went for his phone and dialled 999 with trembling hands. The operator's voice seemed distant.

'Ambulance,' he slurred. 'My wife...'

The rest of the conversation was a blur. He performed CPR as instructed, but everything felt unreal. Images flickered in his mind: his hands squeezing, the shadow figure, something in the darkness using him.

Sirens approached. His daughter Emma was waking. Police and paramedics arrived. He couldn't remember anything that happened, but it was all relived through the bodycam videos played later in court. He held Emma close for as long as he could, shielding her from her mother's body and the activity that surrounded them, before social services took her away. Her tiny fingers gripped his shirt, her eyes wide with confusion that would soon become something worse.

In his cell, detectives questioned him about his marriage.

'It was fine,' he said, though he knew that wasn't the whole truth. He knew they would examine his phone and find the arguments, the terse text messages. He loved his wife, his family, deeply, but love had been distorted into tragedy.

When it came to trial, his confident lawyer, with a tight-lipped smile, cited the 2008 Brian Thomas case. *Automatism*, they called it. In criminal law, automatism can be used as a defence, arguing that the defendant committed an act involuntarily, without awareness or control (e.g. due to a seizure, sleep-walking, or trauma) and therefore lacked criminal intent. The lawyer explained how the brain could be active while the conscious mind slept, allowing complex actions without awareness.

Alan's trial proceeded with expert testimony on parasomnia. The prosecution presented text messages, and a portrait of a marriage in decline. Friends testified to tensions, to Alan's preoccupation with sleep and shadows. Alan was found not guilty due to automatism. His lawyer smiled throughout the deliberation; he knew the precedent would be their saving grace and win him the case. Somewhere deep inside, Alan knew the legal system would fail to capture the truth of that night because the truth defied rational explanation.

There were celebrations, but he cared only about reuniting with Emma. When he finally saw her after nearly a year, the horror of everything broke him. She had grown taller, her face thinner, more guarded. Her eyes, so like Sarah's, regarded him warily. She was having nightmares, the social worker explained, sometimes waking up screaming. Had the shadow now turned its attention to her?

'Emma,' he said, his voice breaking, 'I've missed you so much. It's okay, sweetheart, everything is going to be okay.' But he knew he could never guarantee that false promise.

He sold their old house; it was literally haunted. He found a new home without curtains and a job allowing him to work remotely, spending all his time with Emma. They established new routines. At night, he would tuck her in, read her a story, leave her night light on and the door open, then make sure the cameras and motion sensors were working before going to bed himself in the same room.

Sometimes, watching her sleep, he'd feel a chill, as if something watched from the corners. He dismissed it as the aftereffects of the trauma. PTSD or whatever.

One night, as he watched her, he noticed a darkness deeper than the usual shadows pooled at the foot of her bed. Before he could move, it took shape: the hooded figure.

Cold dread seized him as he realised the terrible truth of his greatest fear: the shadow had always wanted Emma, his miracle child who had once defied death.

'No,' he whispered, 'not her. Take me instead.'

His love was too powerful, the resistance too much, but the debt demanded payment.

'Take me,' he said again, and this time, the shadow did.

4

THE DARK SHADOW

TH WILSON

Bee had invited her college pals around to hers for pizza and beer. Mid-term exams were over, and it was time to chill out, listen to some music or watch a scary movie.

She didn't care so long as exams and revisions weren't discussed or even floated around tonight.

The books and files were hidden away, that bag she had carried for the last ten months was thrown under the bed. The relief she felt at not needing to look at it again for at least another month went beyond fantastic.

Another two years of college, then university, it felt never-ending but she was sure it would be worth it at the end.

Looking around, she walked into her sitting room; it was kind of tidy. An old, saggy grey sofa was against one wall, with scattered beanbags and huge floor cushions. Nothing matched; colours clashed, and patterns were just thrown up everywhere. With everything so expensive nowadays, everyone she knew lived like this and they managed just fine.

A knock at the door brought Bee out of her daze and she opened it to find Lou was first, early for a change, then about two minutes behind her Charly arrived with a crate of beer in her arms.

The boys were paying for the pizza this time, collecting their order along the way.

Catching up on their day the girls chatted about work. Charly was a barista in a local coffee shop. She did three shifts a week; it had been so busy today that the first thing Charly did was take her shoes off and flex her feet as she sipped her bottle of beer, sighing and relaxing into the sofa.

'We had no breathing space. I have no idea what was going on, people were coming out of the woodwork.'

Lou, on the other hand, didn't have much to say. 'Well, I have been lazy, so I read and relaxed today. A real book, not college or work; wonderful. I was so engrossed. It's a ghost story and so good. I'll bring it around when I finish if you want, Bee?'

'Oh, yes please, I love a good ghost story.'

The doorbell went and this time it was pizza. Never mind the lads – pizza time!

They burst in the door, laughing as always. The three of them together were noisy, funny and so lively. When apart, they were quieter and a lot calmer. They were all attractive lads, but to the girls, they were just good friends.

Mark carried the pizzas in and put them on the floor between them. They smelt so tempting and everyone was looking forward to them.

'Toppings tonight,' declared Mark, 'spicy beef and veg, Hawaiian with extra jalapeños and the trusty garlic with extra, extra cheese that we love.' Everyone made a delighted feed-me-now groan, took a slice and settled down with their beers too.

Charly and Lou were on the sofa, sunken but comfortable with their feet up, enjoying their slices and drinking their beers.

Bee had chosen her favourite beanbag. It had images of sushi printed on it and was much more comfortable. She always used this one.

Mark and Si both grabbed big floor cushions, propped them against the wall and settled there for the time being. Greg had used two beanbags, both a bit worn but okay when pushed together.

'Oookaaay, what have we missed, ladieees,' asked Si in a sing-song voice.

'Book talk,' replied Bee.

'Nooooo! Not books or college stuff, remember?'

'Ha ha, you nugget! No, this is a book of fiction, the type you get lost in. Lou is reading one about ghosts and I would like to read it too.'

'Do you believe in that rubbish?' Si pushed.

Charly piped up. 'You don't? What about in your place? It's creepy as hell in there and you've still not told us a thing. Have you seen anything or heard stuff?'

'Woah, girl, woah,' Mark jumped in, 'one question at a time, bloody hell.' He laughed and the rest did too.

'Sorry, I got excited.' Charly giggled around a mouthful of pizza.

They started sharing stories; personal experiences and spooky events and friends' anecdotes. Everyone had a tale to tell, from hearing footsteps to witnessing strange flashing lights as they left or entered rooms.

Charly looked around and asked them, 'Shall we do a séance? Bee, don't you have a Ouija board somewhere?'

Bee was shocked and unhappy at being put on the spot. 'Yes, erm, it's never been used; the box is still sealed. I'm a bit scared of it to be honest. My brother bought it for me as a joke.' Shuddering, she continued. 'Some joke, there's nothing funny about it. But that's Joe for you. He said as I was moving in by myself, I could maybe find some company using it, ha ha... not!'

The group collectively sniggered and then they began talking about using it. Next, they cleared the floor so that they could fit it in the centre and all of them around it.

Bee reluctantly went to find it. She ended up at the back of the cupboard where she stored her shoes and coats – there it was in a black bag, almost hidden out of view.

'I'm not doing it,' she said as she walked back into the room. 'I'll watch and take notes but no way am I touching that thing.'

'No prob,' said Lou and Si at the exact same time.

'Take notes for us, that's a great idea, then we will miss nothing,' Si mumbled as he raked through the box.

Once opened, Greg was grumbling about how it had to be flat so no cheating could go on. They placed the planchette on the board and then looked at each other; all were wondering should they be doing this?

Everyone but Bee was close to the board and they placed one finger on the planchette, ready to begin.

Bee gave them a reminder of the box rules. 'Don't let go of the planchette at any time, no matter what happens. At the end you must say goodbye, you slide it down to the *Goodbye* on the board, don't just say it, otherwise something may follow you home and I do not want anything left here, okay?'

They all nodded, but Greg said, 'For someone terrified you know an awful lot about it, Bee.'

'Yeah, I watch movies, you know, and I read books, forewarned and all that crap. Now choose who's talking to it to start off, then anyone can ask questions.'

They all looked at Greg. He sighed. 'Okay, I'll start, let's move it to *Hello* first and then no one, and I mean *no one* pushes it or moves it again... agreed?'

'Agreed,' they said in unison.

Then they moved it to *Hello*, as instructed and Greg asked, 'Who is with us?'

They waited; one minute... two minutes.

'Nothing.' Charly yawned.

Greg again said, 'Hello, we want to chat with anyone in spirit, can you move this and let us know you're here?'

Nothing...

Greg looked stumped. 'I give up, let's go to *Goodbye* and pack it in.'

They moved the planchette down and all said goodbye, feeling relieved but dejected too.

After a few sighs and nervous laughs, the beers were passed around again, and the lads decided to go to the shop to stock up. More beer and chocolate were on the list.

The girls gave them some money toward the haul and sat

back comfortably and waited for them to return. They chatted about what went wrong and why no one answered. Lou talked about how she had wanted her gran to come through; she missed her and really hoped she would get at least a little bit of contact from her.

Bee nodded and patted her leg from where she was sitting on the floor. 'I had no idea. I'm so sorry you didn't get that, I really am.'

Charly sat up on the edge of the sofa and asked, 'How about a séance instead? Dim the lights, pop a couple of candles on, set the atmosphere; they aren't as dangerous as the Ouija board.'

'They're not as scary, nothing will hang around after a séance. We'll hold hands and think of who we would like to talk to and see what happens,' said Lou.

Bee wasn't so sure but felt she couldn't back out again. It didn't sound as bad. It wasn't like the spirits could talk if she was just thinking of her loved ones. 'Let's see what the lads say once they're back,' she responded.

No sooner did she say this and in they burst.

'Make sure the door's locked please!' Bee shouted over their noise. 'No need for anyone walking in while we're chilling.'

Mark went back through and checked the door was secure, gave a thumbs up to Bee and wandered back in.

Bee felt better knowing it was double-checked. It was after 9pm and dark outside, and she preferred to be locked in; she never knew who was about nowadays, even with the group here.

Lou looked at Bee and then at the rest. She did a little cough then asked who would be interested in the séance. 'We can try with candles and low lights.'

A few shrugs and smiles around beer bottles and it was decided.

Charly pointed to the floor and instructed them. 'C'mon, sit down and let's give it a try.'

They all squashed down and settled on the cushions and carpet.

Greg then took charge. 'Everyone needs to get their backsides sorted now, we could be here a while if that last faff is anything to go by.'

They laughed and then settled into a circle. Charly grabbed the candles out of the bathroom then lit them, placing them in the middle.

'Okay, I've read we need to hold hands, then think of someone we would like to contact. Lou wanted her gran to come through. I would like my brother to chat to me, or send a sign he is happy. I miss him,' Charly told them.

Mark confessed he didn't really have anyone, but he would think of their wishes for extra help, and hopefully that would work too.

Si said he would really like his dad to contact him. Greg admitted it was his gran too, same as Lou.

They waited quietly for Bee, and she sat looking down for a couple of minutes. They all knew it was her mam, she had only been dead a year through cancer, it was still very raw for her.

She sighed and said quietly, 'Mam.'

Everyone nodded and they squeezed the hand they were holding for extra support.

'The lights!' shouted Charly as she jumped up and turned them off before leaping back into her place. It was time.

'Now close your eyes, think of your loved ones and relax, after a few minutes we can talk out loud and ask if anyone would like to come see us or chat if they can, just a little sign from them so we know they are here.'

They all nodded again and agreed with Charly's instructions. They closed their eyes and the deep contemplation of their loved ones began.

No one saw the dark shadow against the wall as it pulsated,

gliding up toward the ceiling. It seemed to time its movements with the steady heartbeats in the room. It stopped in the centre and hovered above them, then continued to undulate and shiver as it changed shape constantly, as if waiting and anticipating.

The room felt colder; they put it down to sitting still and being on the floor. A thin carpet on top of concrete wouldn't keep them warm. The summer was great, a built-in cooling device, but not in winter, lots of extra layers needed. Tonight was not particularly cold, but they were very still, feeling the chill creep up their legs, running down their spines from the air above. No one had realised how the chill had come from above them, how odd that it was from two completely different directions. They were too busy thinking of who they would like to contact.

Charly stirred first. Opening her eyes and looking at them one by one she asked, 'Shall we say their names now and why we would like to contact them? Don't let go of hands though, I am sure it will be stronger if we keep a link between us.'

As they all opened their eyes and got their focus on each other, Charly started. 'My brother, David, I miss you and your cheeky ways, we had lots of laughs together. I am so sorry you were ill, that we lost you so quickly, you know we all loved you, Shorty.' Her eyes glistened as she spoke.

Lou was next to speak. 'My gran, Louisa, my namesake, you looked after me and we had fun days out to the park, I just miss your smile.'

'Dad, you were strict but cool, funny and had a weird dress sense, but hey, you were my dad,' added Si.

'Gran, come say hi, you old misery. No one would believe me anyways,' Greg said, laughing.

Mark shrugged when it was his turn. 'I have no one I miss to be honest. I would love for you all to come to my friends though, thanks.'

'Nice one, very inviting you loser,' Greg said with a smirk.

Mark gave Greg a wink and shrugged again.

Bee was last. She let out a huge sigh as she asked her mam to come say hi. 'I miss you so much, I wouldn't mind a hand with my latest assignment, you were the clever one. Oh, your lasagne too, I do wish we'd frozen lots of that for teatime.' She managed a little laugh between her tears.

'Wicked lasagne chef she was,' agreed Lou.

Then they all looked toward the candles and listened; the only sound was their breathing.

'Can you make a candle flicker or blow one out? Move something or knock on a wall?' Charly asked in a timid voice.

Silence, then a very light breeze sent one of the candles into a dance. No doors or windows were open and none of the other candles had been affected.

Lou whispered, 'I hear tapping over by the door.'

It got louder; tapping, then knocking, and finally banging – travelling up the walls the way the dark shape had earlier, it reached to the edge of the ceiling and stopped.

One by one the candles began to flicker profusely, then they dimmed until, one by one they went out, leaving only one alight and perfectly still.

They were all nervous now, excited too, looking around, gripping hands that were either freezing or sweating. There was an almighty thud on the wall and the last candle went out with a *pfft* as if it had been blown.

They screamed and yelled. Charly jumped up and put the light back on. 'No frigging way did that just happen!' she shouted as she stood with her back against the wall, eyes wide and looking all around the room.

'Definitely wasn't one of us,' Greg added.

Bee was crying, terrified. 'That wasn't family, that wasn't anyone friendly. I want them gone.'

Lou hugged her tight and Greg crawled over to hold them both.

Si and Mark were listening intently and looking all around them.

Even though the light was on, the dark shape was still there... it moved toward Charly. The door beside her was banged on so violently that Charly felt the wall vibrate. She yelped and jumped forward.

Mark leapt up and opened the door and the window. 'Get out now, no one stays here, no one hangs around us, get out NOW!'

They all saw the shape fly across the room from under the door and out of the window.

Stunned and shocked, they stayed where they were, not believing what they had seen and heard.

One by one they made excuses and began to leave, the beer and pizza forgotten.

Greg offered to stay with Bee; he didn't want her to be alone. He liked her a lot, but hadn't told her. Tonight was not the night, but he could show her he was there for her and maybe they could build from there.

They sat on the sofa for a bit longer and chatted about everything except what had just happened. It was too fresh and they needed to mull it over separately before they started dissecting it.

As midnight arrived, Bee decided to go to bed. 'I'll leave the doors open if that's okay, then we can hear each other if we do need anything.'

Greg agreed and settled on the sitting-room sofa, ready for sleep... hopefully.

Bee checked her windows and front door were locked securely, then got changed for bed and climbed under her duvet.

Uncomfortable at first, she looked around her familiar

bedroom, hoping it was safe and clear. She finally started to fall asleep.

As they were both dozing, they didn't see or sense the dark shadow returning and gliding across the sitting room, through the hall and into Bee's bedroom. Floating above her bed and shivering, it reached out and touched her face.

It then slid the blanket off her.

Bee sat up and screamed, and the thing slammed the bedroom and sitting-room doors, blocking them both from getting out.

Terrified, they ran to the doors and tried to open them, yelling at each other to pull and try harder. It was impossible. The darkness had taken control and would only let go when it wanted to. It grew and shuddered as it fed on their terror.

Bee began beating the door with her fists and screaming for help.

Greg grabbed his mobile and tried to ring Si; there was no signal and no way to get help.

They heard a deep laughter and the doors clicked open, slowly and deliberately. Bee and Greg threw them open further and ran to each other. 'Let's get out while we can,' said Greg, panting in the hall.

The doors slammed shut again.

Bee was screaming and hiding her face in Greg's chest. The shadow prevented them from getting to the front door. He couldn't even think what to do and held her close, trying to plan an escape for them.

Then the tapping started; running along the walls and back again, as if it surrounded them, getting louder until it became a thudding that felt as though it was in their heads, it was so violent. They were getting colder and their breath showed; the hall had never been this cold before.

A growing atmosphere built up around them as the silence arrived again.

The front door clicked and opened, but how? They stepped cautiously toward the door and it violently shut again. The shadow was teasing and tormenting them. The walls shook around them as if they were being held and tossed around. Then that disturbing laugh floated above them.

Terrified, they sank to the floor, holding each other tight and keeping as close as they could. They had no idea of what they could do or where to go from here.

The dark shadow hovered in front of them. They watched it; like smoke but more solid, yet it could make shapes as it shivered before them. Neither Bee nor Greg could speak or move, immobile in their terror.

The shadow moved around as if it wanted to touch them but couldn't quite get the energy to do so. Another disturbed laugh sneaked out from behind it.

As it changed shape they began to see things inside it. Bee saw her mam, her beautiful mam crying and fighting to get out of a box. Greg could just make out his gran; she sneered and laughed at him, sitting there scared.

Bee hid her face again and yelled, 'That's not my mam, she isn't there!'

Greg held her close, knowing his gran had been grumpy but not hurtful, not believing what he saw.

The mass moved closer to them and covered them slowly, swallowing up their whole bodies. It felt suffocating and they couldn't move at all.

Suddenly, there was knocking at the front door. A neighbour was shouting for them to open up.

As he got no answer he began to kick it down. Other neighbours were peering out of their doors, and one phoned the police.

As the door broke off its hinges, the neighbour ran inside to find Bee and Greg lying flat on the carpet and seemingly comatose. He began talking to them and shaking them, terrified they were dead. Greg opened his eyes and took a swipe at the neighbour until he realised who it was and that the shadow was inexplicably gone. He turned to Bee, who was still not moving. Greg shook her gently, saying her name over and over, but there was no reaction or sign of life.

'Phone an ambulance, for God's sake help her!' Greg screamed.

The police and ambulance soon arrived and the paramedics tried to wake Bee, but nothing was working. The police took Greg outside and started questioning him, not believing his tall tale.

Bee was taken to hospital, no one knowing what to do to help her. Her heart was beating. But she wasn't there.

The friends met up the next day in a local café. Greg told them what happened. The others had no words. They all sipped their drinks and once finished they left and went their separate ways, unable to cope with what had happened, especially to Bee; all unable to forgive themselves. Greg remained where he was. He had dark bags under his haunted eyes. He was but a shadow of himself.

5

THIN VEIL

NICO

Éamon Byrne's workshop was a small, cluttered space at the back of his cottage in Bruff, a village so quiet it seemed to exist outside of time. The walls were lined with shelves crammed with tools, rolls of leather, and half-finished shoes. A single bulb hung from the ceiling, casting a warm, yellow light over the workbench where Éamon sat, hunched over a pair of boots. The clock on the wall ticked steadily, marking the slow passage of the night.

Éamon, a cobbler, was one of the last of his kind in Ireland. His hands, rough and calloused from decades of work, moved with precision as he stitched the sole of a boot. He was a man of routine, of quiet dedication. His customers relied on him, and he never missed a deadline. But tonight, something felt off. The air in the workshop was heavier than usual, and the shadows seemed to stretch farther than they should.

Éamon set down his tools and rubbed his eyes. The boots were nearly finished, but his hands ached, and his vision blurred from hours of meticulous stitching. He glanced at the clock. It was just past midnight, far later than he usually worked. The workshop felt stifling, the air thick with the scent of leather and polish. He needed a break.

He pushed back his chair and stood, his joints protesting after hours of sitting. The cottage was quiet, the kind of quiet that only comes in the dead of night. He walked through the narrow hallway into the kitchen, the floorboards creaking under his weight. The room was small but tidy, with a worn wooden table, a sink with a few dishes resting in it, and a stove that had seen better days. Éamon filled the kettle with water and set it on the stove, the familiar ritual of making tea a comfort.

As he waited for the water to boil, he leaned against the counter and stared out the window. It was late October. The moon cast a pale light over the village. The wind fluttered against the glass, carrying lingering traces of wood smoke from nearby chimneys. Bruff was asleep, the streets empty, the houses dark. It was a peaceful sight, but tonight it felt... different. The shadows seemed deeper, the silence heavier. Éamon shook his head, dismissing the thought. He was tired, that was all. Too much work and not enough sleep.

The kettle whistled, pulling him from his thoughts. He poured the hot water into a chipped mug and dropped in a teabag, the steam rising in a thin curl. He carried the mug to the table and sat down, the warmth of the tea seeping into his hands. For a moment, he simply sat there, sipping the tea and letting his mind wander. But the attic lingered in his thoughts, a nagging presence he couldn't ignore. There was a tool up there he needed – a small awl he hadn't used in years. He'd been meaning to fetch it for days but kept putting it off. Tonight, though, the thought wouldn't leave him.

With a sigh, he set down the mug and stood. The attic was as good a distraction as any. He climbed the narrow staircase, the wood creaking under his weight, and pushed open the attic door. The space was dimly lit by a single dusty window, and the air smelled of old wood and mildew. Boxes were stacked haphazardly, their contents long forgotten. Éamon began to search, moving aside cobwebs and piles of junk.

It was then that he noticed the box.

It was tucked away in a corner, partially hidden under an old blanket. He knelt down and brushed off the layer of dust. It was unremarkable at first glance, the kind of plain cardboard box you'd find in any attic. But as he looked closer, he noticed symbols scrawled across the lid in thick, faded marker. They were crude but unmistakable – Celtic knots, spirals, and other patterns he recognised, familiar from his connection to Irish heritage and symbols he had seen before. He didn't know what they meant, but they were clearly deliberate, as if someone had marked the box as a reminder of its contents. His curiosity got the better of him. He lifted the lid.

Inside was a turnip lantern – how fitting, with Halloween just a few days away.

It was unlike any lantern he had ever seen. The turnip had been carved with meticulous care, its surface etched with the same intricate patterns marked on the box. The face was haunting – a hollow-eyed grimace that seemed to stare right through him. Éamon picked it up, feeling the weight of it in his hands. It was cold, almost unnaturally so, and the carvings seemed to shift slightly under his fingers, as if alive.

He turned it over, examining it closely. The craftsmanship was extraordinary, showcasing skills that could rival the most masterful works of art. The turnip itself was large, its skin dried and hardened with age, but the carvings were still sharp and precise. He recognised the patterns – spirals, knots, and interlacing lines – symbols of protection and continuity in Celtic tradition. This wasn't just a lantern; it was a relic, a piece of history.

Éamon's mind drifted to the stories he had read about Samhain, the ancient Celtic festival that marked the end of the harvest and the beginning of winter. It was a time when the veil between worlds was said to be at its thinnest, when spirits could cross over into the land of the living. People would carve turnips into lanterns, placing embers inside to ward off evil spirits and guide the souls of the dead. The practice had faded over time, replaced by the pumpkin lanterns of modern Halloween, but here, in his hands, was a piece of that old world.

He ran his thumb over the rough surface of the turnip, feeling the ridges of the carvings. It was strange to think that this lantern had likely been made decades, possibly centuries ago. Who had carved it? What had they hoped to protect against?

And why had it ended up in his attic, hidden away in a box marked with symbols he couldn't fully decipher? The questions swirled in his mind, but there were no answers. Only the lantern, cold and heavy in his hands. It was as if it was calling to him, urging him to light it, to see what it would reveal.

Without thinking, he carried it downstairs, the weight of it pressing against his palms. The kitchen was still warm from the tea he had made earlier, the mug sitting forgotten on the table. He set the lantern down and fetched a candle from the cupboard, the kind he used during power outages. He placed it inside the lantern and struck a match.

The light that spilled out was faint, flickering weakly through the carved holes. But it was enough to cast strange shadows on the walls, shapes that seemed to move when he wasn't looking. Éamon sat back and stared at the lantern, a strange sense of unease settling over him. The flickering light danced in the hollow eyes of the grimace, making it seem almost alive, as if it were watching him.

He told himself it was just his imagination, the product of a long day and an overactive mind. But deep down, he knew it was more than that. The lantern had a pull to it, a quiet, insistent force that drew him in. The carvings seemed to shift and twist in the dim light, the patterns writhing like snakes. The longer he stared, the more he felt as though the lantern was speaking to him, not in words but in whispers that brushed against the edges of his thoughts.

It was hypnotic. The flicker of the candle, the play of light and shadow, the way the grimace seemed to shift from a scowl to a smirk – it all held him captive. He tried to break free, to look away, but his body refused to obey. His hands gripped the edge of the table, his knuckles white, as if anchoring himself against some unseen force. The whispers grew louder, not in his ears but in his mind, a low murmuring chant that he couldn't quite make out. It felt ancient, primal, as if the voices of long-dead spirits were calling to him from across the centuries.

For a moment, he thought he saw figures in the shadows outside – tall, gaunt shapes moving just beyond the edge of the light. They were there and then gone, fleeting as a breath. His heart pounded, but he couldn't move, couldn't speak. The lantern held him, its light pulsing faintly, rhythmically, like a heartbeat. He felt a cold sweat break out on his forehead, his breath coming in shallow gasps. This wasn't right. This wasn't natural.

And yet, part of him wanted to stay. Part of him wanted to listen, to let the whispers guide him. It was a strange, irrational urge, but it was there, tugging at the edges of his will. He clenched his teeth and forced himself to look away, breaking the spell.

The room seemed to snap back into focus, the shadows retreating, the whispers fading into silence. The lantern sat on the table, its light steady and unremarkable once more.

Éamon let out a shaky breath and rubbed his face with his hands. His head ached, and his body felt heavy, as if he'd just run a mile. He glanced at the clock. Hours had passed. The night was deep, and the cottage was silent except for the faint ticking of the clock. The light from the lantern was flickering weakly, casting faint shadows that danced at the edges of his vision.

He wanted to get up, to blow out the candle and leave the lantern behind, but his body refused. His limbs felt like lead, his thoughts sluggish and muddled. The whispers had faded, but their echo lingered, a faint hum in the back of his mind. He rested his elbows on the table and leaned forward, his head heavy. The lantern's light seemed to pulse gently, a slow, rhythmic glow that matched the pounding in his temples.

He told himself he would just close his eyes for a moment,

just until the dizziness passed. But the moment stretched, and the light grew dimmer, softer, until it was nothing more than a faint glow behind his eyelids. The last thing he remembered was the cool surface of the table against his cheek, the faint scent of wax and old wood, and the distant, almost imperceptible sound of voices murmuring in the dark.

The next morning, Éamon woke with a stiff neck and a dull ache behind his eyes. He was still at the kitchen table, the lantern sitting cold and silent in front of him. The candle had burned out, leaving a pool of wax at the bottom. He sat up slowly, wincing as the stiffness in his muscles protested. The events of the night felt like a dream, hazy and disjointed, but the lantern was real enough. It sat there, its hollow eyes staring blankly at him, as if waiting.

He stood and stretched, trying to shake off the lingering unease. The shop wouldn't open itself, and there were boots to finish. He moved through the day on autopilot, his hands working the leather while his mind wandered back to the lantern. The memory of the whispers, the shifting shadows, the way the carvings had seemed to move – it all gnawed at him. He told himself it was nothing, just his imagination running wild. But the thought of lighting the lantern again lingered, a quiet itch he couldn't quite scratch.

By evening, the pull was stronger. He tried to ignore it, busying himself with chores and small tasks, but the lantern was always there, sitting on the table, its presence impossible to ignore. He told himself he was being foolish, that there was no harm in looking at it again. After all, it was just a turnip, carved and dried, nothing more. But deep down, he knew it wasn't that simple. The symbols, the whispers, the way it had held him captive – it was more than just an old relic. It was something else entirely.

Still, curiosity got the better of him. As dusk fell, he found himself standing in front of the lantern, a fresh candle in his hand. He hesitated, his fingers hovering over the matchbox. Was this a mistake? Should he just put it back in the attic and forget about it? But the thought of leaving it untouched felt wrong, as if he were turning his back on something important.

He struck the match and lit the candle. The flame flickered to life, casting its faint, uneven light through the carved holes.

The light was stronger this time, casting longer, more intricate shadows. Éamon sat and watched it, transfixed. The carvings seemed to shift and change, forming patterns he couldn't quite decipher. He felt a strange pull, as if the lantern was calling to him. He didn't resist.

The days blurred together. Éamon's routine fell apart. He forgot to open the shop, forgot to eat, forgot to sleep. His mind was consumed by the lantern. The villagers noticed, of course. They whispered about him, about how he seemed different, distant. But no one said anything to his face. He was the village cobbler, after all. A man they respected but didn't truly know.

On Halloween night, as Éamon sat in his kitchen with the lantern, he noticed something strange. The shadows on the walls weren't just shadows anymore. They were shapes – figures, moving and shifting in the dim light. He leaned closer, his heart pounding. The figures seemed familiar, as if he had seen them before. And then, with a sudden chilling clarity, he realised where he had seen them.

They were villagers.

But not the villagers of Bruff as he knew them. These figures were dressed in old, tattered clothes, their faces gaunt and pale. They moved silently, their eyes fixed on him. Éamon stood up, his chair scraping against the floor. The lantern's light grew brighter, filling the room with an eerie glow. The figures stepped closer, their hands reaching out.

And then, everything went black.

When Éamon opened his eyes, he was no longer in his kitchen. He was standing in the middle of a village, but it didn't look like Bruff. Or so he thought. Éamon stumbled through the village, his breath coming in shallow gasps. The houses around him were unfamiliar yet eerily recognisable. They were smaller, cruder, their walls made of wattle and daub, their roofs thatched with straw. The streets were dirt paths, rutted by cartwheels and dotted with puddles from a recent rain. The air smelled of wood smoke, damp earth, and something else – something ancient and unplaceable.

The people moved around him, their faces gaunt and weathered, their clothes rough-spun and patched. They spoke in a dialect he could barely understand, their words clipped and guttural, their voices carrying a rhythm that felt older than time itself. None of them seemed to notice him. He called out, his voice hoarse and desperate, but they walked past as if he weren't there. He reached out to touch a man's shoulder, but his hand passed through as though he were made of mist.

Panic surged through him. He looked down at his hands and saw they were translucent, the faint outline of the ground visible through them. His heart pounded, but he felt no pulse. His breath came in ragged gasps, but he felt no air in his lungs. Was he a ghost, a shadow, a fragment of something that no longer belonged?

This wasn't *his* Bruff. This was Bruff as it had been centuries ago, a village frozen in a time long before electricity, before paved roads, before the world he knew. The realisation hit him like a blow. He had been transported back, not in body but in soul, to a Hallows' Eve when the veil between worlds was thin, when the old traditions still held sway. Had the lantern done this? Had it pulled him through time, through the thinning veil, and left him stranded here, a stranger in his own past?

He turned in a slow circle, taking in the scene. A bonfire

burned in the centre of the village, its flames leaping high into the night sky. Figures moved around it, their shadows long and flickering. Some carried turnip lanterns, their carved faces glowing faintly in the dark. Others chanted in low, rhythmic voices, their words lost to the crackle of the fire. It was Samhain, the ancient festival he had read about in his books, brought to life before his eyes.

Éamon was trapped, a ghost in a world that wasn't his own. The lantern had called to him, and he had answered, not realising the cost. Now he was here, caught between worlds, a soul adrift in a time that had no place for him. The whispers he had heard, the shadows he had seen – they hadn't been his imagination. They had been the voices of the past, calling him back, pulling him into their world.

And there was no way out.

BACK IN PRESENT-DAY BRUFF, the villagers noticed Éamon's absence. His shop remained closed, the sign on the door still flipped to *Open* as if he had only stepped out for a moment. Days turned into weeks, and still there was no sign of him. Neighbours knocked on his door, calling his name, but the cottage stayed silent. The curtains remained drawn, the windows dark. Eventually, the village moved on, as villages do, and Éamon became another story, a mystery whispered about in the pub on quiet nights.

Months later, new tenants moved into the cottage. They were a young couple, eager to start a new life in the quiet village. The woman, Saoirse, was drawn to the attic almost immediately. She loved old things, the stories they carried, and she had a feeling the attic would be full of treasures. One evening she climbed the narrow staircase with a flashlight in hand.

The attic was cluttered, boxes stacked haphazardly, their

contents long forgotten. Saoirse rummaged through the mess, her flashlight casting long shadows on the walls. It was then that she noticed the cardboard box tucked away in the corner, partially hidden under an old blanket. She knelt down and brushed off the layer of dust, her fingers tracing the edges of the box. The symbols on the lid caught her eye – crude but deliberate, drawn in thick, faded marker. They were strange, almost hypnotic; spirals that seemed to twist inward, knots that looped endlessly, and other patterns she had never seen. She didn't know what they meant, but they felt old, like something out of a history book.

Her curiosity prickled. She wasn't usually one for superstitions, but there was something about the box that pulled at her. It felt out of place, as if it didn't belong among the other clutter. She hesitated for a moment, her hand hovering over the lid, before lifting it.

Inside was a turnip lantern. It was larger than she expected, its surface carved with intricate, almost unsettling designs. The face was the most striking part – a hollow-eyed grimace that seemed to follow her no matter where she moved. The carvings were deep and precise, the work of someone who had taken great care. She reached in and picked it up, surprised by its weight. It was cold, unnaturally so, as if it had been sitting in a freezer rather than an attic.

Saoirse turned it over in her hands, studying the patterns. They were beautiful in a way, but also unsettling. She felt a strange pull, a curiosity that went deeper than mere interest. It was as if the lantern was calling to her, urging her to light it, to see what it would reveal.

She carried the lantern downstairs. She set it on the table, its hollow eyes staring up at her. It sat there, its presence impossible to ignore.

Outside, the days were growing shorter, the nights colder.

The village, as it did every year, was preparing for its renowned Samhain celebration – an event now whispered about across Ireland. But Saoirse hadn't given the holiday much thought – until now. The lantern seemed to hum with a quiet energy, as if it was waiting for her.

After all, Halloween was just a few days away.

6

BEWITCHED?

SUE MOWFORTH

I can pinpoint exactly when the nightmares started.

My long-time next-door neighbours had recently moved and the rumour was going around that their modest bungalow had been bought by a "single woman". As I was one of the few middle-aged bachelors in the village, neighbours had winked at me, as if this was my golden opportunity to get hitched.

I didn't comment. I hate any sort of change and have absolutely no intention of finding a partner.

I've always been a quiet, peaceful sort of person. I keep myself to myself and never cause any problems.

However, when she moved in I was curious enough to sneak a few glances through the bushes at the contents of this "single woman's" removal lorry. In addition to the usual household items were rolls of chicken wire, wooden posts and what looked like various animal feeders.

'So, she keeps animals, does she,' I muttered to myself. 'Hope I'm not going to be disturbed by early-morning cockerels, donkeys braying in her orchard or cats scratching up my flower-beds.'

I watched and noted.

I'd not been sleeping well since my neighbours had left.

Shortly after she moved in, the postman had caught me hiding in the hedge peeping into her garden. I'd heard her digging and was trying to see what she had been doing. She'd put up a washing line against the boundary. I would ask her to remove it. She'd also erected a chicken run. I expected the chickens would smell.

Unfortunately, she noticed me peering through the bushes and invited me round for tea. I felt embarrassed and trapped into accepting. I comforted myself with the thought that it might be an opportunity to bring up the matter of the washing line.

I arrived at 4pm, sharp. She was small with the weathered complexion of an outdoor sort of woman. She stared at me in a way that made me feel uncomfortable. She had an evil-looking cat which glanced at me and ran off.

Apparently her name is Anne.

She led me into the living room. There were boxes all over the place and she apologised for the mess. The room smelt a bit funny. By the window was a parrot chained to a perch and the floor all around was spattered with bird droppings on sheets of newspaper. That explained the funny smell. Most unsanitary. She said that a few years ago the parrot had just flown in and stayed. She had advertised for its owner who had replied and said she could keep it. His wife, who had recently died of cancer, had bought it from a pet shop where it was known for its terrible language and cursing. He didn't want the parrot. Said it needed to be chained to its perch or it would fly off.

So Anne kept it chained up. She'd had two cats but one had died just before she moved here.

She asked what I did for a living. I lied and told her I fixed computers.

That night I had the first of my nightmares. I dreamt that my feather duvet was strangling me.

I woke up covered in sweat and went into the kitchen to make myself a hot drink. There was a full moon so I hadn't needed to put the light on. Peering out of the window I noticed movement in next door's garden. Somewhat alarmed, after all it was a quarter to midnight, I cracked open the kitchen door and ventured outside. Somebody was definitely in her garden. Taking a kitchen knife (I don't know why as I'd no intention of stabbing anyone), I crept up my garden path to where I could see through the hedge. It was Anne dressed in a long robe. I watched as she carried a number of boxes up her garden to the far end of her orchard. Then she set fire to them. Doesn't she know it's strictly against local by-laws to have bonfires in your garden?

I should have shouted out and told her, of course, but it was the middle of the night and what she was doing looked somewhat sinister. From where I was peering through the hedge she seemed to be dancing round the flames. To be honest, I was concerned. In her long robe, dancing round a fire in the middle of the night, she looked like a witch. And witches can put curses on people, can't they?

I decided to creep back indoors and say nothing.

Two days later Anne asked me if I could sort out her computer. I told her I was too busy but she insisted, staring at me with those piercing eyes.

Very reluctantly, I went round. Her laptop was in the lounge. The parrot sat on its perch staring at me without blinking. I couldn't find any problem with the computer but I wasn't able to concentrate with that bird staring at me. It had started making voice-like sounds. Anne came into the room while I was working and apologised for the parrot's language. I couldn't tell what it was saying, but apparently it was swearing at me.

I didn't like going into her house. Apart from the smell there was a bad atmosphere as if I was being watched.

Next day, Anne left three eggs in an egg-box on my front doorstep.

Throwing caution to the wind I used two of them to make an omelette. Later on, I got a headache though I hadn't had a headache in years. I wondered if it was caused by the eggs? I threw the third egg away just in case.

It was the village fête at the end of May. I'd promised, or rather been volunteered to help set out the tables. Cake was handed round. I was given a slice of Madeira cake which seemed all right, but then I overheard someone saying my new neighbour had baked it. I was sick all night. I suspected I'd been poisoned.

Something had been digging in my flower-beds. I kept watch

and saw her cat scratching up my plants. I shouted at it and it ran off. When Anne went out to feed her chickens I told her to keep her cat out of my garden. She said she couldn't control where it went. I told her that she shouldn't have an animal that she can't control.

My headaches were getting worse. I hadn't been able to sleep for days. Was it the summer heat or my nightmares?

A few days later I heard Anne calling out for her cat. She said it had disappeared and asked if she could look for it in my garden. We found it dead under my front hedge. I told her it must have been run over on the road and crawled there to die but Anne seemed to think I was responsible.

The weather had been very hot. Her front room must have really stunk in the heat. I could see the parrot through the bay window sitting on its perch staring out, watching me.

I heard hammering noises through the hedge and noticed she was building what looked like an aviary. I was right. She carried the perch and parrot out of the house and into the aviary. I saw it flying around in there so she must have taken the chain off its leg. I wondered if it would escape. The aviary only had a single door with quite a flimsy-looking catch. I couldn't sleep in this heat. I always keep my windows closed at night, and one night I'd wandered outside briefly where it was a little cooler.

The following morning when I went outside I noticed the parrot had escaped from the aviary and was sitting on top of my garden shed. It stared at me with its evil little eyes and started making its voice noises. I supposed it was cursing me again. I quickly went back inside. Then it flew off.

About an hour later Anne came round, banging on my front door. She looked distressed. She accused me of opening the aviary door during the night. How dare she! What evidence did she have?

My headaches were becoming intolerable. That murdering parrot must have put a curse on me. It had already given cancer to the woman who used to own it, and probably killed both Anne's cats as well. Had it infected me? Was that why I was suffering these horrendous nightmares and headaches?

I made an appointment with the doctor.

I was given boxes of tablets, but I won't take any. They are all poisonous.

I can't cope anymore. I can't seem to think straight. Next door or her blasted parrot are possessed. She's blaming me for everything that's been happening to her and telling people I'm weird. People have started avoiding me. Someone has found the parrot and brought it back. It's still staring at me with those damnable eyes.

The doctor has sent someone round to visit me. I won't let them in. I won't.

Why are the police here?

It's not me they need to see. It's her, next door. Can't they see that it's her, next door, who's to blame? With her evil cats and cursed parrot!

It's not me. It's her and her parrot devil. It's not me!

What's happening? Where are they taking me?

As they drive me away I can see the parrot still staring at me. Its beak is open.

Look. Look! It's laughing at me...

7

CAT WALK

PETER CRICKMORE

The next time I saw the house, high on the hill shielded from the village by a deliberately planted copse, I was taking the cat for a walk. Actually, to be fair to Pansy, what we do is walk together – no self-respecting cat would consent, doglike, to a lead. In fact, it's mostly me following her.

When we set off there was just a hint of rain, so the downpour and a distant rumble of thunder as we emerged from the trees were a surprise. So much so, I didn't recognise the old house as we ran toward it seeking its shelter. Only as I pushed open the elegant, once quite posh front door, did it start to come back to me.

It was the smell that started it – the unmistakeable smell of burnt books sodden in firefighters' failed efforts to control a major blaze. Pansy noticed it too, keeping close as we walked through the large foyer that gave onto the other rooms on the ground floor. There'd been books everywhere, I recalled, all shelved in settings appropriate to their subject matter – cookbooks going back to the eighteenth century in the kitchen, history books on everything in a special room off the kitchen-dining area, music and books on music near a Bösendorfer in the drawing room, science books from Vesalius's *De Humani Corporis Fabrica Libri Septem* and Copernicus's *De Revolutionibus* through to Ken Wilber's *A Brief History of Everything* in another dedicated room.

Was there anything left undamaged, salvageable and missed by looters? I was tempted when a rousing squawk brought me to my senses and Pansy clung to my trousers. I had trodden on Graham, a child's teddy bear, burnt, charred and sodden – and the reason why I knew the house so well: Graham belonged to Nigel, the very best friend of my teenage years. We'd both been to public schools – he to a posh one, me to a very minor one – and, excluded by the locals and ignored by our severe and busy parents, we were naturally drawn together in the hols. We'd fished for carp in his father's ponds, camped overnight in the tenant farmers' barns and had beaten everyone on the estate at croquet.

And we knew the old house better than anyone...

A chilling thought made me shudder. Could it be... was it possible? Dropping Graham, I rushed up the stairway to Nigel's room, the erstwhile nursery. His bed, of course, was a burnt-up wreck, its frame and twisted steel springs testament to the ferocity of a fire that began with Nigel's curtains and spread quickly to the window drapes, cutting off escape from the door. The door itself was not a secret but held one known only to the pair of us. Years ago, we deduced from knick-knacks we found, long before Nigel's family moved in, the door gave onto a narrow passage linking the nursery with a maid's bedroom – a convenience originally for the maid's access to her young charges and later we surmised for the master's access to the maid. At some point – on the insistence of the master's wife, we speculated – the passageway had been blocked off with boards and shelving, to be used by later occupants only as a convenient cupboard. Until we secretly unblocked it.

The secret room became our indoor haunt, where we could come and go, but cunningly arranged we thought so that others casually opening its door would see only shelves stacked with redundant kids' stuff. For us, however, it was a haven – somewhere we hid things we felt grown-ups would not want us teenagers to see or have, where we could make things either of us could take to school to impress our friends. On one occasion we even smuggled two girls in for an otherwise innocent kissing session. Why we didn't use the secret room rather than the spacious nursery for our experiments with indoor fireworks, I can't imagine.

Pansy and I stood for minutes staring at the charred door that had once been a recourse and refuge from parental authority. She shivered, her nose pointing toward the long-abandoned entrance. I shivered too, wondering if Nigel had not actually escaped as I had assumed; if the firefighters had also been deceived by our toy shelves, assumed the door led only to a cupboard and consequently moved on to quell flames in the next room. They would have unknowingly left poor Nigel, trapped when the flames were at their height; he would have retreated to the secret room – but not from the smoke and heat.

Nigel, my best friend of my teenage years, the friend whose loss was so profound I'd deliberately excised him from memory whenever I returned home for holidays; could he still be there behind the door? Or his corpse?

I picked up Pansy and fled as I had on that fateful day, out through the parents' room, down the stairs two, sometimes three, at a time, out into the rain and across the meadow to the trees, whence Pansy had brought me.

I must have collapsed there because it was nearly dark when I woke, Pansy licking my face. Together we continued down the hill to my parents' cottage.

The ground, like my clothes, was dry.

And no, my mother confirmed, there had been no rain for weeks.

8

TAKE CARE

LES WOOD

'All right, Bobby?' It was Clarke, the foreman, on his way out of the compound.

'Aye, no too bad,' Bobby replied.

'Last night the night then, eh? Whole shebang comes doon the morra. Will ye hang aboot tae watch it?'

'Nah. Don't think so. Ah'll be ready for ma kip by then.'

It was Bobby's last night on this job. He'd spent the last five weeks as night watchman in Barbour Court, a derelict block of flats due for demolition – scheduled for blasting the next day. The explosive charges were already in place, all the way up to the eighteenth floor. All that remained was for the specialist guys to link them up to the detonating electronics tomorrow morning, and the whole tower would be coming down about eleven o'clock. There would be big crowds, of course, with everyone pushed way beyond the safety lines, and a party atmosphere, a sense of excitement at seeing something so vast and monumental being brought to its knees.

'Got anything else lined up for after this then?' Clarke asked, rubbing dust from his eyes.

'No yet,' said Bobby. 'Ah'm hoping ah might be able to get something on they new housing developments. Ye know, six or eight months on the one site, nae real bother, just patrolling the houses every couple of hours.' He looked up at the tower block looming above them. 'Not like this bloody lump. Boring isnae the word for it.'

Clarke glanced up at the tower and shrugged. 'Aye, well, it'll no be here much longer. See ye in the morning.' Clarke hitched his jacket over his shoulder and strode out of the compound.

Bobby Thomson turned and walked toward the tower block, passing the other demolition workers as they made their way out and home for the night. Clarke was really the only one who talked to him. The rest of the men barely grunted a recognition, even if he caught their eyes directly. He suspected they looked down on him – the janny, the budgie, the old watchie. Couldn't hold down a real job.

Let them think what they like. To hell with the lot of them.

He met Dawson coming out of the entrance to the flats.

'Wee Bobby Thomson!' shouted Dawson, throwing a couple of fake shadow-boxer punches at him. 'How're ye hanging? Me and a couple of the fellas are going for a wee celebratory swally doon the Swan. Just tae raise a glass tae honking auld Barbour Court.' Dawson tilted his head back to look up at the flats. Strips of wallpaper and ragged curtains fluttered like pendants from the broken window frames that clung to the crumbling brick-work. 'Minging dump!' he shouted. He turned back to Bobby, looked him up and down. 'Pity ye're stuck in here all night though. Shame ye cannae come!' Dawson laughed.

Bobby hated Dawson. He was Bobby's daytime counterpart, a much younger man, supposedly looking after the site during the working day, but mostly just hanging around with the demolition crew, joking and laughing, lending a wee hand here and there. He got on well with the other men, who all seemed to like him. He was a nasty piece of work though, with a cruel streak in him. Bobby had heard stories about how Dawson could be particularly vicious if he caught any kids on the site. He didn't just shout at them to clear off, but snuck up on them, grabbing them tight by the arms and twisting till they cried. Or kicking them so hard on the backside that they lifted right off the ground. Just wee weans. Clarke seemed to let Dawson get away with it though. 'They weans'll know no tae come back,' he'd said. Dawson was more cautious with the bigger lads though. He usually got somebody to help him see off any of the older neds who sometimes wandered onto the site looking for something to steal and sell later. No, Dawson was too scared to tackle *those* guys on his own.

Bobby hated Dawson for another reason. Dawson treated

him as if he were some retarded fool, speaking down to him, kidding him mercilessly about his individual habits, the way he kept his overalls spotless, the Westerns he liked to read. Bobby was only the *night* watchman. Not the highly responsible and totally indispensable *day* watchman. No, somebody like Bobby could never be qualified enough to rise to the heights of Dawson's day watchman post.

What an idiot.

Bobby scowled at him. Dawson looked as though he'd already started with his celebrations. He didn't look too steady on his feet. Just as well it was his last day on the job or Clarke would probably have fired him there and then.

'Hey, c'mon, wee man!' Dawson shouted, gesturing to the gate of the compound. 'Ah'm the last. Let me oot so's ye can lock up for the night.'

'Are ye sure ye're the last?' asked Bobby. 'Ah don't want anybody else coming oot after ye're away. Once ah'm locked up, that's it.'

'Aye, aye, aye,' said Dawson. 'Ah'm the last. Don't get het up aboot it. The rest are already in the pub. Ah made sure ah was last so's ah don't have tae buy the first round.' He grinned. 'Or the second for that matter. Ah should've two pints of heavy lined up waiting for me when ah get there. And ye're holding me up! C'mon, shift it!'

Bobby turned and followed Dawson to the gate. The whole site area had been cleared earlier that day in preparation for the demolition tomorrow. All the heavy plant, all the salvageable material that had been lying around had been removed, leaving just the empty space of the compound covered with a thin film of brick dust. Both men kicked up clouds of red soot that swirled and eddied around them.

Dawson went out and closed the gate behind him. He watched through the chain-link fencing as Bobby padlocked the gate. 'Well, that's me finished. Don't suppose ah'll see ye again. Ah start a new job on Monday on one of they new housing estates. Ten months' work. Magic!'

Bobby stared at him grimly. 'Very good,' he conceded.

'Anyway, ah'm away. Get maself well and truly blootered. But just remember, wee man.'

'What's that then?' Bobby asked. He knew what was coming.

'Take care, noo!' Dawson bellowed, and dissolved into loud guffaws. 'Take care!' He turned and walked off down the street, wiping tears of laughter from his eyes, and shaking his head at how hilarious he was.

Bobby glowered. 'Ah'll take care all right,' he muttered to himself.

It was one of Dawson's tall stories. He'd told it to a few of the men on the first day of the demolition contract. Bobby had been there that day, since all the site workers were expected to be in attendance for a briefing from Clarke, laying down the rules and regulations of site discipline and conduct. Dawson had gathered a few of the men around him at one of the tea breaks, telling dirty jokes and playing cards. Bobby had stood at the back of the Portakabin sipping his tea.

'Here,' said Dawson, 'have ye heard the story aboot this place?'

'What story's that then?' replied McCulloch, a burly, unshaven man in filthy dungarees.

'The one about how the caretaker in these flats was killed?'

'On ye go then,' said McCulloch. A few of the men looked at each other and smiled.

'Ah swear tae God it's true,' said Dawson. 'Ah heard it from a wee wifie at the shops up the road. Happened aboot twenty years ago.' He settled back in his chair, scanned the faces of the men, watched them nudging each other as they settled down for a good yarn. Dawson let the silence hang for a few more seconds and went on. 'Seems the caretaker, Eddie Jamieson, was a wee bit of a scatter-brained guy. Always hashing aboot doing wee odd jobs here and there. Helping women with their washing and looking after the weans while they went oot tae the shops. This was back in the days when the caretakers actually lived in the flats, mind. Anyway, this guy always tried tae dae his own repairs in the flats. If a boiler went, or one of the spin dryers packed up in the ground-floor laundry, Eddie would be yer man tae dae a running repair till the electricians or whatever managed to have a look at it.

'Well, one day, one of the lifts went on the blink. Nae problem tae Eddie, he'd managed tae get them restarted loads of times before. Saved waiting for the lift engineers to come oot. What, with wee auld women on the top floors and that, it was easier tae dae it himself. This day, the lift was stuck between floors – ten and eleven, ah think it was. So Eddie goes up tae eleven, opens the doors and he can see the lift sitting there just below the level of the floor, three or four feet down maybe. So, he gets oot his toolkit, and lowers himself doon onto the roof of the lift. He opens up the control box that sits on the roof and buggers aboot a bit with the switches and things. He's done this kinda thing afore. Loadsa times. After a wee while, he thinks he might have got it fixed, and he presses the start button on the roof box. Nothing happens. He tries again. Still nothing. He's sure it should be working, so he presses the start button again, and then jumps up and doon on the roof to kinda bump-start it, like. Christ almighty, does the bugger no lurch intae life and start up with him still on the roof! He completely lost his balance and fell onto his back. By this time the lift had moved up and was level with the open doors on the eleventh, and Eddie slipped, half on, half off of the lift roof, his body hanging oot of the landing doors. But the lift kept going. It didnae stop. Just kept going up. Poor Eddie got his body trapped at the top of the landing doors, with the lift still pushing up. Very near haufed him in two, so it did.

'He lasted for sixteen hours after it. Poor bugger. It just goes tae show ye. He was the caretaker... but he didnae take enough care, eh? Didnae take care!' Dawson laughed.

No one else did. The other men shuffled in their seats and looked away. Bobby thought maybe they'd seen too many accidents in their time to laugh at something like this.

'Aye, ah've heard that story too, son,' said McCulloch, getting up and moving to the door. 'And it isnae funny.' McCulloch glared at Dawson. 'Right?'

'Oh, aye.' Dawson's face reddened, and he swallowed hard. 'Er... Ah didnae mean anything by it, ye know. Sorry.' Dawson had looked straight at Bobby at this point, fixing him with a fierce glint in his eye, as if to say, *Don't you even think aboot bringing this up again*.

Bobby didn't have to. Dawson did it himself. Every night. Just as he was leaving, and Bobby was locking up, Dawson would shout over the street to him, 'Take care noo!' and burst into a fit of giggles. It was as if he felt he could reassert his authority over him by showing he didn't care what Bobby thought of his story. Bobby was not one of the gang, never had a pint waiting for him in the Swan.

Bobby didn't count.

Bobby thought the man was a moron.

He cast a long look at Dawson's back as he headed down the street to the corner. *Look at him*, he thought. *A nae-brain who could manage tae talk his way intae any job, even one in a new housing development*.

He turned and trudged back to the tower block. It rose above him, a grim tombstone soaring into the darkening sky. No cheerful twinkles shone in the windows for the homecoming worker or the urban prisoner. No fond kisses waiting at the door.

No smells and sounds of cooking teas, news on the telly, weans playing in the stairwell. Just black, blank, mindless eyes staring out at the city.

Still, this was the last night. It would all be gone by this time tomorrow, reduced to a three-storey pile of rubble which would get cleared away brick by brick, memory by memory to some landfill site at the edge of the city.

Bobby stood outside the entrance hallway. The light was fading fast now, the clouds lowering in from the west obscuring the little that was left of the late autumn's gloaming. He went over to the little generator that crouched like some deformed animal at the doorway and turned the starting handle. The electricity supply for the building had been disconnected weeks ago and the generator was hooked up to give some juice to the ground floor in order to light the small security office where Bobby spent his nights. It took three tries before the generator finally spluttered into life. *I hope those idiots have left enough petrol in it*, he thought.

He went through into his little office. It was not much more than a cubby-hole, converted from one of the original airing cupboards which serviced the ground-floor laundries. It didn't contain much; a small desk, a chair, a two-bar electric fire and his radio. There was a portable television as well, but Bobby didn't like to watch it. It was Dawson's, and besides, there was never anything worth watching in the wee small hours.

He sat down and took out his lunchbox – he called it lunch, except it was usually about ten o'clock at night when he ate it – Mary had made it up for him earlier. A couple of gammon sandwiches, a packet of tomato sauce crisps, a Twix and a flask of tea. *No much of a feast*, he thought.

He placed his food on the desk and rummaged in his bag for his book. He loved Westerns – couldn't read enough of them. He managed to get through one book roughly every two nights, buying up dozens at a time at second-hand bookshops and car boot sales. This particular one – *Outlaw Guns* – wasn't that good. Pretty much formula stuff. Bobby considered himself a connoisseur of the Western. Could do Western book reviews for *The Herald* or *The Scotsman* if he wanted. He threw the book onto the table, took his jacket off and hung it on the hook on the door. He noticed that Dawson had left another one of his porn magazines on the floor under the desk. He picked it up and looked at the cover. Bobby shook his head. He flicked through the magazine, barely glancing at the pictures.

He threw the magazine in the bin, settled down in his chair, feet up on the desk and stared at the ceiling. He thought of all those empty floors above him, silent, dark and calm. He felt a tinge of sadness at the thought of it all coming crashing down tomorrow, this vast warehouse of memories. Thirty years the tower had stood. He thought of the flats, each wall reverberating with the tiniest echoes of everything that had ever happened in them, fading in an unending diminuendo, but still there all the same; the conversations, the shouting, the playing, the fighting, the sex, the eating, drinking, sleeping. The banging.

The *banging*?

He snapped out of his fantasy and listened intently. No doubt about it. He could hear something banging. He'd become used to the sounds the tower could make at night. The low howl of the wind in the two hundred foot organ pipe that was the central stairwell, the small tinkle of loose masonry and plaster as it drifted and tumbled down in the spaces of the wall cavities, the general creaks and groans as the building cooled and settled in the night air. But this was different. Something way up there, very quiet, but regular and insistent nonetheless. *It could be weans. Somehow sneaked in. Or... wait a minute. Some bugger's got locked in. Dawson was in too much of a hurry tae get oot tonight. Some guy has probably been left on one of the floors. Locked in.*

Probably been sleeping on the job. Blootered, maybe. Locked in. Aye, that's probably it.

'Good Christ,' he said with a sigh. 'Aye, all right, all right, ah'm coming.' He picked up his torch and made his way to the stairwell. Nothing for it but to climb – no power for the lifts.

Out in the stairwell it was as black as the Earl of Hell's waistcoat and the wind was picking up, causing the tower to wail in tormented protest. He flicked on the torch and flashed its beam up to the half-landing leading to the first floor. He could still hear the banging, but it seemed a bit quieter here, perhaps dampened by the wind. It sounded high up. *Nine or ten, maybe,* he thought. It was hard to tell. He'd only been up to the first floor before, when Clarke showed him the layout of the flats. Two flats on either side of the stairwell, with two lifts, one serving the even floors and the other the odd floors.

His torch beam carved out a wide cone in the floating dust of the stairwell. Beyond, it was inky black.

He started his climb. When he got to the first-floor landing, he realised this was going to be harder than he thought. Thirty-one stairs he'd counted – fifteen to the half-landing and sixteen to the first floor. *Bugger it.* He was getting too old for this – this was going to take it out of him. If there *was* somebody banging away up there, he'd better have a damn good excuse for being here.

His progress was slow. At each landing he'd shine his torch around, inspecting for any signs of life. Each floor looked the same; grimy, rubble-strewn floors, abandoned boxes and plastic bags, cables tangled like dead snakes in the corners. The banging had definitely got louder though. It seemed to be getting faster as well.

He arrived at the seventh floor. He was sure now that the banging was coming from the floor above him. It was reverberating down the stairs, causing the glass of the doors leading to the flats to shake and judder.

He hesitated. What if it wasn't someone locked in? What if it was vandals, trying to wreck something, steal some lead piping. Drug addicts? He'd already had to chase a few during the last couple of weeks.

He thought about Dawson's story. What if…? *Don't be daft*, he told himself, laughing. *Right then, let's see what this is all about*. Galvanised by his determination to put ghosts out of his mind, he pushed up quickly to the eighth floor. His heart thudded heavily in his chest from the effort. This was definitely it. The banging was from here somewhere.

'Hello!' he shouted. 'Ah'm here. Where the hell are ye?'

The banging continued, an echoing, metallic sound. He shone his torch around, sending shadows dancing and lurching across the stairwell.

Nothing.

He swallowed dryly and went over to the doorway leading to the left-hand group of flats. This seemed to be where the noise was coming from. The door was battered and splintered, and it hung from its hinges like a drunk clinging to a lamp-post. He shone the torch into the hallway, scanning along the wall. Something was moving to his left and caught his eye. He swung the torch back, and laughed out loud in relief.

There it was. The waste disposal chute. This was used by the residents to get rid of their rubbish without having to troop down to the bins in the basement every time. They simply emptied their rubbish into the hatch and it dropped down the chute, running parallel to the lift shaft, to empty into four or five large bins in the basement of the tower. The hatch door had come loose and was rocking back and forward on its hinges, banging against the chute entrance, powered by the high wind no doubt.

Bobby went over and pushed it shut. There was a strange sucking sound, like a sudden intake of breath, followed by a deep, deep silence. He was startled by the stillness, felt it settle on him like a shroud in the blackness. He turned his torch to look at the doors to the two flats in the hallway. Meshed glass panels, shattered and punctured, they both still had their name plates – *Bowie* and *Carlin*.

Something moved behind one of the doors, a scuttling low figure, and his heart punched against his ribs. He forced himself to look again. There was nothing but shadows. It was just an illusion. A reflection from his torch beam. Curtains flapping in the wind. Nothing more.

It dawned on him that he was standing here in almost complete darkness, in the very middle of the tower block. Ten floors above him, seven below. It was eerily quiet; even the wind had dropped, causing the banshee howl of the stairwell to shrink and withdraw to a low murmur. He wasn't easily scared, but he realised he was letting his imagination run away from him. The torch beam added to his unease. He could only pick out small details of the landing. Whatever the beam fell on – a power socket in the wall, a curled edge of linoleum on the floor, a spider-crack in the glass doors – it emphasised the surrounding dark rather than relieved it. It unsettled him.

He switched the torch off.

Total blackness.

'What the hell did ah do that for?' he said, the sound of his own voice making him jump. He switched the torch back on again, but it wouldn't light. 'Aw, no,' he moaned. He tried again, banging it against the wall. Nothing. His pupils dilated, widening to their maximum, seeking any stray photon. He shook the torch hard, thumping the battery casing with the heel of his hand. At last it sprang into light.

As it did so, there came the unmistakable sound of the lift

machinery starting up. Somewhere among the floors above him. Up there in the dark.

Right, that was it. There *was* some idiot in here! He was right the first time. *I'll bet it's that wee eejit Dawson and his mates, come back tae wind me up*, he thought. *I'll bloody well show them.*

He pushed through into the stairwell and sprinted up, taking the steps two and three at a time. Nothing on nine. Up past ten, and coming up from the half-landing onto eleven, he could see a faint glow from the hallway on the left-hand side. *There's the idiot*, he thought. *That'll be the light from the lift. Ah'll bloody get him now!*

It was only as he pulled himself up, exhausted, onto the eleventh-floor landing that the realisation hit him as if the entire tower block had collapsed on top of him, burying him under its suffocating weight.

There was no electricity.

There was no way the lifts could be running. Had they reconnected it? No, he would have been told and, besides, the demolition was tomorrow. What the hell was going on?

He slowly shone his torch over to the right-hand hallway. He could see the beam shaking against the wall as his hand trembled. There was no doubt about it. There was a light coming from in there. He could still hear the sound of the lift machinery. It sounded strained, whining, high-pitched against the background of the wind. And there was something else. Was that a voice? He thought he could hear a voice, a low moan. He walked over to the hall door and slowly pushed it open.

Without warning, the torch went out.

He stopped, his hand on the door-handle, his heart hammering against his chest. It suddenly got very cold. His breath, coming in rapid gasps, steamed in the air before him. To his right, he saw the lift door was open. From within, a thin, bleak light oozed out. The lift slowly rose and fell, clanging and whining as the machinery struggled to raise the weight a few inches then collapsing back to start again.

He jumped as the torch suddenly came back on. He shone it over to the lift and saw something flapping up near the top right-hand corner. An oily rag that looked like a hand flopped out from above the lift door. Or was it a hand that looked like an oily rag? He tried to swallow but couldn't. He had no saliva left. He heard a moan coming from the top of the lift. On the roof.

He stood back against the wall, his legs shaking, and shone the torch into the small space between the roof of the lift and the door-jamb.

He thought he saw a face. Somewhere back there was a face. A man's face.

The lips were contorted in a snarl of pain and fear. Eyes stared out at him, directly into his own; probing, seeking, pleading.

He closed his own eyes. *Christ*! He couldn't bear to look at it any longer. The wind groaned in the stairwell, and it seemed to find its echo in the lift shaft. It sounded like a voice. So soft, so low. Had he really heard it? It came again. *Help me, please.*

He looked up.

Into the deep dark at the top of the door. Into the shadows where something was moving. Way back in there.

He shuffled toward the lift, his legs barely able to take his weight, and watched his hand stretch out, reaching up toward the rag that tumbled and danced from the top of the lift.

As he touched the cloth he felt icy fingers close around his own; tight, sickeningly tight, and pulling him in.

Pulling him in.

THEY'D HAD to cancel the blasting, of course. Man unaccounted for and all that. They found him three days later. It had been

Dawson who thought of looking in the lift shafts, finding the crumpled body, twisted and buckled at the bottom of the odd shaft. He must have fallen from a fair height. Nothing to break his fall. The lifts themselves had been taken out the day before Bobby was last seen. The other men were sad to hear the news of the body's discovery, but they soon got on with the job in hand. Time was money.

Only Dawson seemed more affected than most. Clarke noticed him sitting off to one side, his back to the perimeter fence of the compound. He walked over to him.

'Don't take it too hard, man,' he said. 'Accidents happen every day.'

Dawson didn't look up. He sat there, turning something over in his hand again and again, staring at it unblinkingly.

Clarke squinted at the object. It was some sort of rag. 'What have ye got there?' he asked.

Dawson kept his head down but held the thing out for Clarke to see. 'He was holding this,' said Dawson. 'Holding it tight in his hands. Where the hell did he get this? Eh? Tell me that, Clarke.' He looked up and there were tears in his eyes. 'Where in God's sweet earth did he get this?'

Clarke took the object from Dawson and examined it. It was an old electrician's glove, oily and ragged with years of wear. He turned it over. On the wrist was a label, once white but faded now to a grimy grey. Something had been written there; the ink, leached out into the fabric by damp and sweat, running in a scrawled smudge across the label. Clarke held it closer to read the words.

He frowned and looked at Dawson.

'Who the hell is Eddie Jamieson?' he asked.

9

THE BARN

JANE MORGAN

So, just to be clear – I *don't* believe in ghosts: once you're dead, you're dead – that's it – fiery furnace, heavenly clouds or a great big nothingness. You've shed your mortal coil; you don't come back; you've moved on.

Let me explain why.

Back in the day, when I was nine to be exact, I had a holiday on my grandad's farm – what a place! His cows had names like Buttercup, Daisy or Gertrude. A ginger-and-white Hereford called Butterscotch was my favourite. They had the sort of eyes that you could lose yourself in – golden brown with thick lashes. His flock of sheep grazed the Welsh hillside and took loud exception to the sheep dip each spring. Grandma's chickens gurgled and crooned on their nests and *mostly* let you put your hand beneath their feathers to gather lovely warm eggs, though I was traumatised on one occasion by one pecking me for being so importunate. But – it was the sheepdogs who had my heart. Like nine-year-old me, they were permanently restless: their eyes watching every move, feathery tails thumping the ground, ears cocked for the tiniest sound. They were a mother, Sweep, and a son, Sooty. I expect you can tell I was allowed to name them, but they *did* have really black coats. They crouched on all fours ready to obey to the letter Grandad's whistles or commands; *hold, come by* and the like. They could kettle and drive those sheep, objecting vociferously, to the gate in minutes, darting side to side behind their waggly tails. His flock knew exactly who was in charge.

There weren't toys or games as such to occupy me: feeding the cows, collecting the eggs and playing with Sooty and Sweep was more than enough. You could always get them to jump for a stick above their heads or scrummage for a bit of dinner left-overs – no Winalot for these farm workers. Some days older cousins visited, so we'd play in the outbuildings or scrump kidney beans, apples, or gooseberries from the little cottage garden. They obviously tasted much better scrumped because they were illegal contraband. Grandma would *not* have approved; the fruit were for pies after the Sunday roast, not for rampaging children. Obstacle races with the hay bales in the barn was a popular option. You could vault over, creep through a gap, walk along a very uneven hay-bale wall. I know it's a cliche to say we made our own amusement in those days, but it was absolutely true. It still is my "safe place" when I feel depressed, can't sleep or whatever.

Anyway – enough of the idyllic memories – all tinged with a healthy dose of nostalgia I do realise – the mention of the barn brings me to The Incident.

Cousins, June, aged ten, and Johnny, aged eleven, were visiting and hide 'n' seek was the game of choice. My turn to hide and the cow-shed and henhouse had been done – so I scurried into the cool darkness of the barn and settled into a little hay "nest" behind some bales. Sooty had decided to join me, so we burrowed down together. The sun slanted through gaps in the roof, catching wisps of straw and dust motes. I watched them drift about in the slivers of light, cuddled up to Sooty's warm, wavy coat and my eyes started to feel very heavy. I could hear 'Seventeen, eighteen, nineteen, twenty. Ready or not, I'm com-ing!' chorused outside and I stroked the dog's head to quieten him. I needed to be found last or I would be the seeker again.

It was warm; I was tired and, like the dust motes, I drifted off – I know I did.

...I was in total darkness – a cave perhaps. I stretched out my hand to feel what was in front of me but couldn't see my fingers. The blackness was intense, enveloping and cold, *so* cold. I shivered and froze as a voice came out of the darkness and whispered close to my ear. I could feel breath on my face and I flinched. A chill ran down my neck. I tensed.

'Help me!' whispered the voice. It didn't sound human – too faint, too ethereal. 'Take me with you. Take me back to the light.'

My breath was coming fast. I was panting, heart racing. I couldn't speak, no sound, no words.

Then – oh God – a hand, well... something... seized my forearm. I felt – what? – claws possibly, but the lasting impression was being held by icicles digging into my flesh. I whimpered, trying to tear my arm from the creature's vice-like grip. I lashed out with my other arm and then pulled myself free. The "thing" slithered backwards, hissing hopelessly, 'To the light, to the light,' which turned to desperate sobbing. It's a sound I can never forget.

Anyway – deep breath – at this point, the barn door opened and Sooty stopped his plaintive whimpering and dashed out into the sunshine, into the light. I screwed my eyes tightly and tried to find my way back from the cave as June and Johnny made a great pantomime of not being able to find me – then – lo and behold – their faces appeared over the bales!

'Look at you – all snuggled up in your hay nest,' June began; then stopped. 'You all right, Jake? You look a bit – well, weird – to be honest.'

I yawned and stretched theatrically. 'You two took ages to find me. S'pose I dozed off for a second...'

'Ooh – yikes – what have you done to your arm? You've got a great blue bruise and some horrible scratches. Sooty didn't do it, did he? He shot past us, tail between his legs and went straight to his mother. He's having a comforting lick from Sweep at the moment, his head snuggled under her paw.'

I looked at the livid marks running from my wrist to elbow. 'Nah,' I remember saying, 'just scratched myself on some straw, I reckon.'

Johnny, head cocked, looked at me searchingly, then grimaced and shrugged. 'Whatever you say, Jake... Probably time to go in anyway. Let's go eat Grandma's famous shepherd's pie and see if we can wheedle our way onto the milk round tomorrow – that's always good fun.'

'What's the matter with Sooty?' Grandad said over some Welsh cakes later that evening. He rubbed the dog's ears, frowning. 'He seems twitchy and doesn't usually settle by my feet.'

Grandad's human antennae were rubbish, but the man was finely attuned to his dogs.

'Don't know,' said Johnny. 'He's been a bit spooked since finding him in the barn with Jake.'

'The hay barn?' said Grandad thoughtfully. He raised an eyebrow at Grandma, knitting steadily by the fireside opposite him.

Taking her cue, Gran turned to June, the responsible one. 'I thought we said not to go in there when the bales were stacked.'

'Ye-es,' June looked earnest, 'but we're always really careful. We don't climb or anything.'

Grandma looked sceptical, then sighed and said, 'You know the people we bought the farm from?'

Johnny nodded. 'The Turners. Got on a boat to Australia soon after selling up, you said.'

'Quite right.' A pause. 'As far away as possible, everyone thought. Well, it was because of what happened to their little daughter, Emily. They found her in there one afternoon – dead.'

The single syllable hung in the air. June and Johnny stared across the table meaningfully.

'They think,' Grandma continued, 'she'd been climbing because she'd heard a creature snuffling about or perhaps to see whether she could touch the roof when the hay had been harvested and stockpiled.' She paused again. 'Anyway, the poor little mite must've fallen and was found broken, lying on the floor of the barn. I don't like going in there much myself,' she admitted. 'It brings it all back...'

We were silent, staring at the tablecloth, imagining the small child scrabbling at the straw for a handhold, slipping, falling through the air...

June looked at me, horrified, and mouthed, 'Those scratches!'

I just shrugged, carried on reading my *Just William* book.

I'd had a bad dream, that was all. It was dark in the barn, so, yes, it was dark in the cave. There was breath on my face; but then Sooty was really close. I heard whimpering in the cave; well, the dog was whimpering at the barn door. My subconscious was just weaving everything together. It can all be explained perfectly rationally. A vivid dream, a couple of scratches on an arm and a whimpering sheepdog do not a ghostly encounter make.

So, as I said, personally, I *don't* believe in ghosts.

I didn't play much in the barn after that though – a bit cold.

10

GALLERY

JACK WRIGHT

Olivia's grandmother, Ethel, was almost completely unremarkable, and if it weren't for the box of photographs sat on Olivia's table, nobody would even remember what she looked like. Ethel had spent the last few months of her life in a trance – dementia, the doctors had said, and Olivia would have believed them, if it weren't for the slight glimmer of recognition in her eyes when Olivia came to visit. No, Olivia had told herself it was something else, something she was keeping secret, like a poker hand, kept close to the chest.

Olivia remembered the last proper conversation she'd had with Ethel, before the silence took hold. They'd been looking through one of the photo albums together – the one with the red leather cover and gold-leaf edges.

'Such a shame,' Ethel had said, her finger trembling as she pointed to each face, 'all of them gone now.'

'Gone where, Gran?'

Ethel had looked up then, her eyes sharp and focused in a way Olivia hadn't seen for weeks. 'Some things are better left alone, dear. Some things should stay in their frames.' Then she'd snapped the album shut and refused to look at another photograph again.

The box of photographs was the only thing Ethel had left behind. After the funeral, Olivia had endured a parade of legal appointments where men in suits competed to look the most solemn, as if they'd known Ethel at all, while they dissected her grandmother's life into bullet points and bank statements. In the end, they simply dumped Ethel's belongings, which turned out to be the box and only the box, into Olivia's lap.

Evening light cut through Olivia's apartment window and landed squarely upon the box, which had been sat on her living-room table now for a week. The apartment was designed to contain exactly one life, no more, no less – a carefully curated space of whitewashed walls and trailing plants, where every coffee cup and throw pillow had featured in at least one sponsored post. Vintage camera bodies lined the windowsill, though they were more aesthetic than functional these days. The irony wasn't lost on her. Olivia sat in front of the box, finally deciding to go through the old lady's belongings. Inside, she found scattered trinkets, tarnished jewellery, and a thick stack of photographs bound by a rubber band that had gone brittle with age.

Olivia spread the photographs across her table. Here was Ethel at a winter wedding, there at a beach house in Cornwall, each image showing her grandmother's slow transformation from black hair to grey. She paused at a garden party photo, something catching her eye, or rather someone. The photo was typical of the era – ladies in floral dresses clutching champagne flutes, men in summer suits discussing business, children chasing each other through perfectly manicured flower-beds. But there, partially obscured by a rose bush heavy with blooms, stood an older gentleman. His clothing was all wrong for the scene – a trilby hat pulled low over his brow and a Victorian-style suit that looked too heavy for the summer day, the fabric so dark it seemed to create a void in the cheerful gathering. He was facing away from the party, as if deliberately turning his back on the joy and laughter captured in the moment.

Olivia looked closer at the photograph but the details were blurry. Taking her phone from the pocket of her ripped jeans, she aimed the camera at the photograph and clicked the capture button. She composed a message to her mother.

Any idea who this is?

She went to attach the photo, but something looked different. The Gentleman was now facing the camera. She looked back at the photograph from the box. The man's eyes now met hers. Olivia rubbed her forehead. *Wasn't he facing away earlier? I'm not sure now.* She hit send regardless.

The phone vibrated against the wooden table.

No idea, never seen him before.

Olivia thumbed through more photos. The Gentleman appeared in each one, his gaze now unmistakably fixed on her. Beach holidays, Christmas mornings, birthday parties – he was there in every scene, a dark smudge of wrongness against the happy memories. Sometimes half hidden behind trees or doorways, sometimes standing bold as brass among the party guests, but always watching, always waiting. She returned to the pictures she'd already examined. There he was in every single one, his eyes piercing through the photographs and into her skull, each appearance slightly closer to the foreground, slightly more in focus.

He's in every photograph.

She thumbed urgently at the phone, and hit send once more.

Weird. Maybe just a friend of Ethel?

Olivia took this into consideration for a moment, before responding.

Every photograph though?

There came no reply.

Olivia spent that night hunched over her laptop, the glow of the screen turning her face ghostly in the darkness. She'd started with the obvious searches: *man appearing in old photos*,

Victorian ghost in pictures, strange figure photographs. Most results were obviously fake – teens with too much time and Photoshop on their hands. But one forum thread caught her eye.

My grandmother burned all our family photos before she died, the post read. *She kept saying something was wrong with them. That something was getting closer.*

Olivia's fingers hovered over the keyboard. She could ask for more details, could tell them about The Gentleman. But what if talking about him made it worse? What if, like a virus, he spread through words as well as images?

She closed the laptop. The forum post had been dated three years ago. The user had never posted again.

The next morning, Olivia was getting ready for the day. She spent an hour perfecting her signature look – dark hair carefully tousled to seem effortlessly messy, winged eyeliner sharp enough to cut glass, and a vintage dress that had cost three weeks' worth of sponsored posts. Everything about her was designed to look accidental, from her chipped burgundy nail polish to the tiny gold nose ring that caught the light just so.

She walked down to the street, ready to take a photograph of the day's outfit. Olivia had built her following carefully over the years. Each morning's photo was a production – the right angle, the right light, the right casual lean against exactly the right brick wall. Her followers called it authenticity. Olivia called it work. She knew every shadow on her street, every splash of interesting graffiti, every blooming flower that might add that perfect pop of colour to the background. But today, staring through her phone's screen at the empty street, something felt different. The familiar corners felt darker, the shadows deeper. She adjusted her pose and tried to shake off the feeling.

Bring on the day xoxo.

She attached today's photo and hit post. Almost immediately, it had gained dozens of likes and comments. One comment snagged her attention.

> Who is the creepy guy behind the car though lol.

She inspected the photograph. There, slightly off in the distance, stood The Gentleman. She looked at the spot where he had been stood in the photograph, but there was nobody there.

She held up her phone once more and took another photograph.

The Gentleman was there again. She looked over at the spot where he was standing – still empty.

This isn't right, she thought to herself.

She attached the photo to a message to her mother.

> Now he's in my photo? WTF?

No answer. Olivia walked to the tree at the end of the road and took another photo of herself. The Gentleman was there. This time, though, he was slightly closer.

Olivia's thumb hovered over her phone's camera button. Part of her needed to know if he was even closer now, but another part remembered the look in her grandmother's eyes during those final months – that wasn't dementia dulling her gaze – it was fear.

Olivia's hands trembled as she forced herself to take one more photo. The Gentleman had halved the distance between them, his Victorian suit now crisp and clear in the image. The fabric seemed to shimmer like oil on water, too dark to be real black, moving in ways that cloth shouldn't. His face was contorted into a smile, wide and unnatural, stretching past where a human smile should end. The skin around his mouth was cracked and grey, like old photographs left too long in the sun. She deleted it immediately.

She returned to her small apartment and opened her grandmother's box of photographs on her living-room table. Each smiling family scene now felt like a lie – how long had he been watching? How had Ethel known to keep this secret?

She took another photo.

The Gentleman was now here, in the apartment with her.

He's in my home.

It felt like a violation.

That does it, she thought.

Olivia retrieved a metal bowl from a kitchen cupboard and began to look for something flammable. No flammable fluids, but Olivia remembered reading something on the internet. She took a cotton ball and a tub of Vaseline, smearing the cotton ball into it. The ball ignited with a single strike of a match, the flame dancing higher than she expected. She dumped several of these cotton balls into the metal bowl and dumped the photos on top. The collection went up in flames easily, faster than normal paper should burn. The edges of the photographs curled and blackened, and for a moment, Olivia swore she could see The Gentleman's face in every photo simultaneously, all of them smiling that terrible smile as the flames consumed them. The smoke alarm went off, its shrill beeping making her jump, and Olivia was forced to move it all to the street.

Once the old photos had turned black and ashy, Olivia held up her phone once more and took another photo. She hesitated to look at it, worried about what she might see. She took a breath, and opened the photo. The Gentleman was now only a few feet away from her. His thin hair seemed to spike out from underneath the hat at odd angles. That smile was still there, that awful, sinister smile.

Olivia attempted to call her mother, but there was no answer.

Okay, if he can see me through the photos, she thought, *maybe he can hear me too.*

She raised her phone once more, set it to video mode, and hit record.

'Okay, man in the suit, what is it you want?' She paused for a moment, giving him time to answer, if he answered at all.

'Is there something I can do to make you leave?' She paused for a beat once more.

She stopped the recording and opened the video.

The Gentleman stood in silence just over Olivia's shoulder, watching her as she recorded, unmoving and just watching with that sinister, horrible smile. His hair appeared as though it was floating underwater, each strand moving independently against gravity, like dark seaweed in a current. Although he was smiling, his eyes conveyed no emotion at all, like a gargoyle on an old cathedral – just empty black circles that seemed to absorb light rather than reflect it. His suit rippled without wind, the fabric moving like something alive. Olivia watched as she asked her questions, with the man completely unfazed by her whole ordeal, his presence a tear in reality that shouldn't exist.

Olivia's phone rang. It was her mother.

'Mum, that man—' started Olivia, but her mother interrupted her.

'He's here,' her mother whispered. 'I took a photo of my garden, that man is stood there. Every time I take a picture he gets closer.'

Olivia's blood ran cold.

'Delete the photos, Mum, delete them now!' cried Olivia.

'I did, Olivia. It doesn't matter. He's here now!'

The line went dead. Olivia looked at the phone screen.

Hundreds of notifications lined the screen, comments and likes from social media.

> Who is the creepy guy?
>
> Is that a ghost?
>
> What's with the man in the hat?

Oh my God, thought Olivia, *they can all see him now.*

Her finger hovered over the create post button. She'd typed and deleted the warning a dozen times.

> About the man in my photos—

No, that would only make them look closer.

> Warning: please don't look too carefully at my recent posts—

That would just make them curious.

Her notifications kept buzzing:

> Love the creepy guy in the background! Is this like an art thing?
>
> That Victorian ghost edit is amazing! How did you do it?
>
> Getting serious horror vibes from your latest aesthetic!

Each new comment felt like a nail in a coffin. They thought it was a filter, a clever edit, some new viral marketing campaign. Her followers were sharing the images, analysing them, zooming in on The Gentleman's face.

She started deleting posts, but it was too late. Screenshots were already circulating. Fan accounts had reposted them. Her

DMs were flooding with people asking how she'd achieved the effect.

DAY 3 OF TRYING TO FIGURE OUT @OLIVIASLOOKS CREEPY VICTORIAN MAN EDITS, one follower tweeted, alongside a heavily filtered photo. In the background, barely visible, stood The Gentleman.

'Stop,' Olivia whispered to her phone. 'Please stop sharing them.'

But social media was doing what social media did best – making things go viral.

Olivia lay in her bed, holding her phone above her face. The darkness of her room felt different now, heavier somehow, as if the shadows themselves were watching her. Her curtains moved slightly in a breeze that didn't exist.

She had to know.

'If anyone sees this, it's my last video,' she told the camera, her voice shaking despite her attempts to steady it. 'There's something in the photographs. If you've seen him too, I'm sorry. I'm so sorry.'

She stopped the recording. She had to know, her curiosity was too strong. She hit play.

The Gentleman was lying beside her, hair floating in and around his face like seaweed in the ocean, each strand writhing independently as if trying to reach for her. His suit seemed to merge with the darkness around them, making it impossible to tell where the fabric ended and the shadows began. As she watched, a grey hand with impossibly long fingers, skin like ancient paper, reached for her neck.

The phone clattered to the floor.

11

FRAMING MILDRED

DAVID J AITKEN

Mildred heard her before she saw her. A female voice calling out, '*You're so beautiful.*' So direct was the address that she felt a hot tingle of embarrassment fill her cheeks, unsure why someone would seek to pick her out like this. She was disappointed when she realised that the only person nearby was the fat bald bloke manning the stall she was browsing. He caught her eye, arching a single suggestive brow.

She looked back down, refocusing on her potential purchases. She had been thinking that she would try and do a deal on a plastic tub filled with decorative thimbles sitting amongst the man's other jumble on an old wallpaper-pasting table. '*I love your red hair, it's so luscious,*' the voice called out again. This time when Mildred looked up her eyes fell upon a painting of a girl. She was hanging on the open rear door of the man's ancient yellow Transit van, parked up behind his stall. She wondered if somebody could be hiding in there, trying to wind her up for some reason, but it was too full of stuff for anyone to fit. She gazed again at the girl, who for the briefest moment appeared to return the look. A *Mona Lisa* illusion, Mildred thought. She sized up the painting, taking in the image, understanding the technique employed by the artist. Struck by just how fantastic she looked, Mildred dropped the idea of buying the thimbles, figuring that this painting could be today's king piece. It was a portrait, like those kitsch ones of Chinese girls by that Russian artist, Tretchikoff. This wasn't one of these though, and it wasn't of a Chinese girl. She was Scottish. A warrior queen from the time of Wallace and Bruce by the looks of her get-up, and Mildred was pretty sure she was an original. She was beautiful, the girl. A proper stunner, as her mum would have described her, had she still been around.

Mildred sensed the seller watching her. She switched her attention back to the thimbles, eager not to show her hand. She picked one up and gave it a studious going-over. Mildred had developed strategies for buying at the car boot sale. The key to getting what she wanted for the price she wanted was not to go for the king piece straight away. If somebody was selling something really good, a nice bit of china or some antique furniture, Mildred's method was to soften them up a bit first. Spend a couple of quid on an old pub ashtray or a beer tankard, get the seller feeling good about her because she had already passed money their way. She picked up one of those old dollies in a crocheted dress that folk used to hide toilet rolls under – proper tat. She quickly agreed a price of one-fifty with the man. The next item in her buttering up game was a bit more expensive. A decorative plate commemorating the silver jubilee of Queen Elizabeth. The greedy seller wanted a tenner for it. She went in low with a three quid offer. He played hardball and in the end she reluctantly forked out seven-fifty. She'd chuck the toilet roll dolly, but she could hopefully get fifteen quid for the Queenie plate on eBay. He'd also been happy enough to sell some of the thimbles individually, so she'd bought two for a fiver. More potential online resale profit to be had. She'd passed enough money his way that it was now time for her to go in for the kill.

'Erm, how much for the painting?'

'A real beauty that one, isn't she?' He smirked, daring Mildred to try and buy her.

'Aye, it's nice... *unusual.*'

'Two hundred quid.'

'What? Get lost. You're having a laugh.'

'No, love, no jokes here. Although if you really wanted one, I'd be willing to throw it in for free, if you pay the full two hundred for the painting. I do a good line in knock-knock jokes, as it happens.' He chuckled, a hearty fat man laugh.

Right weirdo this one, Mildred thought.

'I'll give you forty for the painting.'

'Sorry, love. It's two hundred, no negotiating.'

Nobody pays two hundred quid for a painting at a car boot sale, ridiculous sum of money. Normally she'd walk away at this point, force him to reconsider her offer as he watched her and her dough disappear off into the distance, but instead he turned his attention away from her to ask a young lad who was flicking through a box of vinyl if he'd seen anything he fancied. It was a deliberate slight. She considered for a minute just grabbing the painting and doing a runner, but she was a semi-regular at this car boot sale. She'd need to be smarter than that.

Mildred wandered around other stalls for a while, browsing, but not really. All the time she was pretending to look at stuff, picking items up and turning them round as though to inspect them, her sights were fixed on the painting. '*Come back, you're the one,*' she swore she heard the girl call out to her at one point across the expanse of the old factory goods yard.

He seemed to be doing a roaring trade, the seller, his knick-knacks and bric-a-brac attracting a constant stream of interested browsers and buyers. Mildred figured her painting was safe for now, no one was going to fork out for the girl at such an inflated price. At another stall she placed the jewel-encrusted trinket-box she had been pretending to be interested in back down onto the seller's table and picked up some other piece of tat. Looking up again, she watched as the man turned round to his van and lifted the painting down, letting a wee old wifey in a headscarf get a closer look. Mildred watched as the woman held the warrior queen above her, angling the painting so she could see her in the best possible light. Mildred wiped a hand across the back of her neck, the collar of her bristly winter coat rubbing against her clammy skin. Surely the old woman wasn't going to pay the full two hundred quid asking price.

'You want to make me an offer for that, sweetie?'

'Eh, sorry?'

A middle-aged woman, reclining in an old deckchair next to

the open boot of her hatchback, pointed at the item in Mildred's hand. All the while a sausage dog sporting a tartan body warmer snoozed on her lap. 'The vase. Would you like to make me an offer?'

'Oh, no. Thank you.'

She placed the piece of pale-blue seventies' glassware back onto the woman's table and headed over again to the stall with the painting.

'Please yourself,' the woman said, as Mildred scooted back across the yard, her urgency jarring against the languid mass of Sunday morning browsers. Mildred slowed to a stroll as the woman handed the painting back to the man; a rush of relief soothing her previous panic. She had the two hundred quid on her in cash and was now considering just paying the rip-off merchant what he wanted. But then the old woman reached around, pulling her long-strapped handbag across her hip, lifting its flap to retrieve her purse. *Shit.* He began to wrap up the painting, bagging it over and over in a series of different plastic bags, tying it off with a piece of string. The woman handed him a pile of notes and he handed her the painting. *Her* painting. As the old woman turned and departed, he looked up and saw Mildred's dejection. He waved the wad of notes at her. She flung him two fingers and walked off.

Mildred wasn't done yet. She followed the old woman all the way out of the car boot sale and back onto the main road until they reached a bus stop. She hung back, watching as the woman waited. There was nobody else around. The thought of snatching the painting came to her again. It wouldn't just be robbery though, she'd be done for assault too, if she was caught. She was becoming overly invested in the fate of this piece of art, but her need to have the painting had now ramped up to something approaching lustful desire rather than just aesthetic appreciation. She heard the girl in the painting again, through the layers of plastic bags, singing a sorrowful lament, inviting Mildred to come close and know her.

The bus pulled up. A number seventy-five heading for Castlemilk. The opposite direction from where she lived. She'd come this far. Mildred followed the woman onto the bus, tapping her card on the reader. The woman took a seat in the front half of the single-decker. Mildred, feeling bold, picked the adjacent seat across the aisle. The bus trundled on, a few more folk getting on at the next stop at the big supermarket.

'You been at the car boot sale then?' Mildred piped up.

'Aye, hen, I have that. Got some cracking bargains.' The woman beamed.

'I love the car boot sale,' said Mildred, 'used to go with my mum every weekend. She's not here now, but I keep going myself. She always loved to try and find that special something in the middle of all the junk.'

'Aye, it's like a treasure hunt right enough. You need a bit of knowledge and sharp senses to come out on top though. Have you got a good eye then, hen?'

'I like to think so. What I do every week I go is I look for two things: quality craftsmanship and something with a good story behind it. If you can find an item that's got both of those then you're laughing.'

'That's clever, hen. I think I might have managed that with my big piece today.' She tapped the frame of the wrapped-up painting, sitting upright on the seat next to her.

'Oh, what's that you've been buying?'

'This? Oh, she's a real beauty this one, so she is. She's my newest girl, the latest one to join my collection.'

'It's a portrait then is it? Do you collect them?'

'Come on, hen, you know fine well what she is. We all saw you looking at her at Charlie's stall. You wanted her pretty bad, we all could tell.'

Mildred was embarrassed by the accusation, but also weirded out by the description of a collective “we” of watchers.

‘Yeah, I was quite taken with her, I suppose. But Charlie, is that his name?’ The woman nodded. ‘He was asking too much for her I thought.’

‘Art is valuable, darling, but then a piece is only worth as much as someone is willing to pay for it.’

‘Do you mind, can I ask what you paid?’

‘I paid the full price, ’cause I know what she’s worth.’ The woman tapped the frame again.

‘Who do you think she is then, the girl in the painting, or who was she, I should say,’ asked Mildred, changing the subject.

‘She’s an is, most definitely, not yet a was. As far as I can remember.’

‘So, she’s a portrait of someone you know?’

‘Oh yes, I know her all right, just like I know all my girls.’

‘Your other paintings, you mean?’

‘Oh yes, I know them all intimately.’

‘And you buy them all at car boot sales?’

‘Oh no, no, I paint them all myself, I’m the artist you see.’

This made little sense, why would she be buying one of her own paintings at a car boot sale? Before Mildred could grill her any further on the revelation, the woman had pressed the stop button and was gathering up her handbag and painting in readiness to get off.

‘This is me now, hen. I tell you what, do you want to come up to my place? I could introduce you to my girls. I think they’d like you.’

‘Erm, okay. That would be nice, thank you.’ Mildred, intrigued, stood up and followed the woman off the bus.

Approaching the flat’s front door, on the top floor of a six-storey block, Mildred was out of breath. The lift out of order, she’d had to stop on the way up for a rest. Not the woman though, who had galloped up each flight, so by the time Mildred had reached the flat the woman had taken off her coat and was waiting for her by the door in a figure-hugging floral red dress. She had also removed her headscarf and appeared to be far more youthful and indeed beautiful than she had seemed on the bus. Wavy raven hair cascaded around her shoulders framing intense angular features.

'Won't you come in?' Her blue eyes beckoned Mildred into the flat.

She nodded and stepped past her into the narrow hallway, its walls lined with portraits of girls. Mildred sensed their eyes on her, following her progress through the hallway. '*Be careful,*' she thought she heard one of them whisper. She heard the woman click her fingers, as an impatient parent would to an errant child.

'Straight ahead, on you go, hen, through to the kitchen. Let me make you a cuppa.'

'Thank you, that would be lovely.'

'Take a seat. I'll get the kettle on.'

Mildred took off her coat and sat at the dining table by the bay window. 'Great view.'

'Aye, hen, it's fab isn't it? Herbal tea okay for you?'

'Lovely, thank you.'

'My own blend,' she said, reaching for a caddy and spooning the dried leaves into a balled infuser.

'Did you train at the art school then?' Mildred asked, spotting an easel wedged between a section of wall and the fridge-freezer.

'Oh no, hen, I'm self-taught. Don't set much store in those kinda places, that's a sort of indoctrination they've got going on there. Institutions, hen, they're all the same. I'm not one for rules. I enjoy breaking them too much, if you catch my drift.'

Carrying a tray across with a teapot, a cup and saucer, and a glass of water, the woman set it down, before taking the seat next to Mildred.

'We'll let that sit for just a wee minute.'

The woman lifted Mildred's resting hand from the table and cradled it between her own.

'So, tell me about yourself...'

'Erm, what do you want to know?'

'What's your name? That's always a good place to start.' She smiled at her, squeezing her hand.

'Mildred.'

'Mildred... Mild and red, eh?' She chuckled. The woman stroked Mildred across her freckled cheek with an extended digit. 'Such a lovely complexion, and I do love your curls.' She twirled a strand of her red locks around her forefinger. 'I'd like to paint you, I think. What say you, Mildred?' She cupped Mildred's jaw in her hand as though inspecting her bone structure. 'Don't answer just yet, this should be almost ready.'

Mildred watched as she lifted the lid from the teapot and swirled the infuser, ensuring the steaming water was fully imbued with flavour from the leaves. She replaced the lid and poured the tea. The smell was sweet and exotic.

'What's your name?' Mildred asked.

'Why, I'm Anne.'

'Anne the artist?'

'That's right. You are a sweetheart.' The woman lifted Mildred's hand and kissed it.

Anne's intimacy with Mildred was a comforting reminder of her own mother, another tactile and affectionate woman. Anne slid the cup and saucer toward Mildred. 'Drink up, my dear.' Anne raised her glass of water and sipped.

Mildred lifted the floral cup to her lips, blowing a delicate cooling breath across the liquid's amber surface, before taking a sip. The richness of its scent was more than matched by the tea's flavour. An image of an ornate Eastern palace with a beautifully dressed princess padding across marble floors in soft velvet slippers formed in Mildred's mind.

'Yes, yes, I think that would suit you perfectly, Mildred.' Anne was immediately excitable. 'An Indian princess, perhaps. I have just the sari for you, it's a deep dark green, which I think would complement your colouring beautifully.' Anne bounced to her feet. 'You stay here and finish your tea. I'll go and set up the studio.'

Mildred continued to sip on the tea. She felt very relaxed and giggled as she thought of the odd turn her day had taken. '*Leave. Leave while you still can,*' said a voice from the far end of the kitchen, but by now Mildred was too caught up in her own thoughts to hear the warning from another of Anne's girls, sat high on a cluttered shelf amongst a jungle of trailing pot plants.

Ushered into Anne's studio, at one time the flat's living room, Mildred stood in a daze as Anne undressed her. Carefully folding her clothes, she laid them on the cushioned leather seat of an antique wooden dining chair. Despite the chill, standing now in only her knickers, Mildred was perfectly relaxed. Normally she wouldn't be comfortable displaying her nakedness to a stranger, but Anne had a way about her that put Mildred at ease. Besides, she was now only partly present in the room of the sixth-floor flat. In her mind Mildred was standing on the marble terrace of a huge palace gazing upon a glorious sunset.

Anne returned to the room with a green sari folded over one arm. She began to dress Mildred. 'You have a lovely figure, my dear. I think the painting would be all the better for revealing some of your naked beauty.' She draped the sari across her shoulder, but left a single breast exposed. 'Come sit down over here, Mildred.' She led her to a chair positioned in the middle of a large white cyclorama. Anne lifted a Grecian-style pillar into the background of the scene. On top of it she placed a full and vibrant, green-leafed aspidistra in a Chinese-style pot. Finally, she rested a clutch of orange-flowered gladioli along the length of Mildred's arm, parallel to the sweep of the sari, the long stalks of the flowers held in her resting open palm. 'There. That's perfect. A beautiful princess.' She kissed Mildred's forehead.

Mildred, now fully transported to her new palace setting, looked out across a lush lagoon, where a vast flamboyance of flamingos preened and postured, their calls echoing across the gentle waters. So far away was Mildred, that when Charlie, the seller from the car boot sale, stuck his head round the door, commenting to Anne, 'Great job, love. She's going to be a real beauty that one,' she was utterly oblivious.

With the paint dry, Anne mounted the portrait within a carved gilt frame. Around the same time, Mildred's focus returned to the flat. Becoming aware of where she was again, she felt a giddiness. She was being carried from Anne's studio back into the hallway of the flat. All around, a chorus of moans and whimpers reverberated within the narrow passageway.

'Enough. Cut that nonsense out right now,' a man's voice barked.

Floating there as Anne held her, Mildred watched as Charlie (*Wait, what the hell is he doing here?*) hammered a picture hook into the wall. Happy with its positioning, Anne passed Mildred over to Charlie, who took her in both hands, looking at her with that same smug smirk he had first given her when she had asked the price of the portrait of the warrior queen. As he hung her on the wall, beautifully framed and sitting against a backdrop of the purest white marble, so Mildred glanced across to see the warrior queen hanging on the wall directly opposite. Eyes full of sadness, she mouthed the words, '*I'm so sorry*.'

. . .

The following weekend at the car boot sale, Barbara, having laid out all her bits, sauntered over to Anne and Charlie's stall, Wilfred, Barbara's sausage dog waddling behind. Still setting up, the couple's distinct yellow Transit van was parked in its usual spot.

'Oh,' said Barbara, 'who's the redhead?'

'She's my best one yet,' said Anne, looking up at Mildred, 'even if I do say so myself.'

'Aye, Barbara, she's a real beauty that one,' said Charlie.

'You two are terrible, so you are.'

As the trio laughed, a tear rolled from Mildred's eye, trickling down the canvas.

12

THE SECOND BETWEEN

EWAN KIRKWOOD

There's nothing to see. All is emptiness.

In the centre of the emptiness is a pool. The liquid is thick. Syrupy. It is warm and transparent. It slowly expands. There's nothing beneath the puddle, nothing but the emptiness.

Scattered around are wooden blocks. These rectangular objects have colourful designs, like you'd find in a child's playroom. They're large and dense. The slowly seeping liquid reaches one of the blocks and wraps around it. The green block stays firm as the sludge swarms it, forming a small moat.

A brightly coloured chair with rusting wheels resides further into the emptiness. A rollercoaster cart. The bulky seat has the over-the-shoulder restraints found in a theme-park ride, one of which is locked downwards.

Beneath the rollercoaster seat is a second pool of translucent liquid. This puddle isn't spreading as quickly as the first, as though the rollercoaster ride has its own gravitational pull, holding the liquid close.

Bobbing in front of the cart is a silver balloon. The balloon is anchored by a string, tied to the seat. The string vanishes beneath the carriage's wheels. There's no wind. No weather. Yet the balloon sways in place.

Finally. This emptiness feels full. Not because of the liquid, the blocks, the cart, or the balloon. Because of the people.

A young woman lies slumped in the rollercoaster seat. She's restrained by the safety harness. Her head is limp against the balloon. It is unaffected by her weight and props her up.

A man in his early twenties, Josh, lies flat on the ground. His head lies squarely in the centre of the puddle of translucent liquid.

This could be it. This time it might be perfect. It has to be.

JOSH WAKES from a sleep he hadn't realised he was in.

How did he get here? Why was he asleep on the ground?

He props himself up onto his elbows with a pained grunt. His head is wet and warm. With one hand he pats the wetness. He drags his hand along his face, removing whatever excess liquid is plastered there. When done, he still feels a dampness. There's no liquid there, he'd just cleaned it off.

'What?' Josh says.

He jumps onto his feet. He rubs both his hands vigorously across his face. He scrubs and scrubs, but the feeling of something wet lingers. Resigning to the fact that the wetness is too deep in his pores and in his hair to remove, he drops his arms with a sigh.

Josh glances to where he'd just been lying. There's something there. He'd hardly noticed it before. It was borderline invisible. Exactly where his soggy head had been lying, is a pool. It looks like water. It moves outwards, a sludgy progression. He has no idea what kind of water could look and move this way.

Dropping to his knees once more, Josh leans close to the substance. The closer he gets, the more confused he becomes. It looks like still water; it's not bubbling. He sniffs the air. He can't quite put his finger on the smell, though he knows he's smelt it before.

Josh rolls up the sleeve of his BAPE hoodie. If he's going to touch the stuff that's currently soaking his scalp, he's not ruining a £300 hooded sweatshirt.

'What's the worst that could happen, Joshy boy?' he asks. Nobody hears.

With a deep breath, Josh sticks his hand into the liquid. His hand glides through the goop, as if he isn't touching it. He lifts his hand up. There's no dripping, no wetness. There's no anything.

He tries again, dipping his hand into the substance with more confidence than before. He can't feel anything as he swirls his hand around. The liquid doesn't splash as he slaps his hands off it. He spits into it but his saliva flies through the liquid and onto the ground beneath it. Yet it doesn't. The bubbles of spit he'd produced all but vanished when impacting the strange goo beneath him. Is there even ground here?

Josh gawks at it, tilting his head as a confused dog would do. He realises something. It hadn't even crossed his mind until now. There's no reflection. He's been gazing at this see-through puddle all this time but it hasn't stared back.

'What is this?' Josh says.

He gets back to his feet and scratches his soggy scalp. His head is hot. It isn't burning from the inside, not like the migraines he's always suffered. It's like a hot-water bottle is strapped to his head. And it's leaking.

There's a noise. A groan. A female voice.

Then Josh remembers who he had been with before. Beth. He can't see her; he can barely see a foot in front of him. He has to find her. He hopes she makes another sound. She does.

A scream.

Following his ears, Josh takes off. He collides with something heavy. A striking pain jabs into Josh's right foot as he loses his balance mid-stride and collapses to the ground. His fall's uncomfortable landing causes him further hurt.

Swearing at whatever tripped him, his eyes fix on a large wooden block painted pink. It has a crudely drawn monkey eating a banana on it. If he finds whatever kid left a block that size around here, he'll give them a piece of his mind. He has half a mind to toss it away.

He'd heard Beth scream. She can't be far. He pushes himself upright and moves as quickly as his stinging foot allows. Limping, Josh notices dozens of the colourfully painted children's blocks all over the ground. Avoiding the strong temptation to volley them away, he presses on.

Josh's legs struggle to lift. He feels as though he's underwater.

Seconds pass between each step he takes. It's like this place is stopping him from moving. He roars into the nothingness in blatant frustration.

A shining foil balloon comes into view. It is floating in the air, bobbing around. Josh reaches out toward the balloon, grasping its string. It doesn't move under Josh's weight. It feels like an iron girder. He gawps at it, confused. Somewhat grateful that the balloon is stabilised, Josh leans against it to regain his breath.

He scratches at his head again. Why is it so wet?

'Hello?'

The words come from nearby. Nearby yet so far away. It's Beth's voice.

She's close now. Josh looks around, still hardly seeing anything. Her voice sounded an arm's length away. He reaches out, his hand piercing the emptiness. He flaps it around whilst balancing himself on the anchored balloon.

'Beth? It's me. Can you hear me?' Josh shouts.

'Josh?' comes the disembodied sound.

'It's me, baby,' Josh exclaims.

Something brushes Josh's hands, not quite making contact. Josh spins his whole body toward it. He propels himself up and off the weighted balloon and leaps toward what he'd felt.

Appearing out of nowhere comes an elaborately designed chair. It looks like a rollercoaster ride, plopped into the middle of this place. A cart with no tracks. It is primarily a neon orange, with splashes of other luminous paints across its body. It is a two-seater, but only one of the seats is in use.

Sat in the left rollercoaster seat, with the U-shaped over-the-shoulder restraint trapping her in, is Beth. She is frantically pushing at the colourful restraint, trying to free herself. She looks flustered. But still beautiful.

Josh runs to Beth. He places a hand on her face. Without

words, they look at each other before kissing deeply. He holds her head and rubs his fingers through her hair, which is all over the place, as if she's been on an actual rollercoaster ride. That's not like her, she always keeps herself neat.

'What's going on?' she asks.

'I have no idea, baby,' Josh replies.

'Well, where are we?' Beth says.

They both pause and look around them. All Josh sees is the rollercoaster seat, the foil balloon, scattered wooden blocks, and two puddles of strange goo.

'I don't have a clue,' Josh says.

'Okay, well, get me out of this chair,' Beth demands. She tries again to lift the restraint off her shoulders. Still it doesn't budge.

Josh joins in, yanking at the metal handles on the restraint. Even with both of them pulling, it still doesn't open. Josh groans, then makes his way around the side of the rollercoaster car. Fearing that he'll trip or get confused again, he keeps one hand on the large body of the cart. He does a lap all the way round it, seeing no obvious lever, button, or switch which could be a release latch.

Beth doesn't take that news well. 'Get me out of this chair, Josh! And get this balloon out my face.'

'What do you think I've been doing?' Josh snarls.

'Don't get snippy with me. It's probably your fault we're here,' Beth retorts.

Their relationship had always been fiery. Beth's friends warned her about dating a guy like Josh. A stereotypical bad boy was hardly a match for a prim and proper young lady.

Josh dropped out of school at sixteen, worked in his dad's garage, and before long had earned enough for his own car. An old banger with enough modifications to stand toe-to-toe with new sports cars. Aside from Beth, it was Josh's pride in life.

Beth was a straight-A student with half a dozen unconditional offers to prestigious universities across the country. A chance meeting with Josh outside his dad's garage changed the course of her life, around a year earlier. She still worked hard in her final year at school but also lived a lavish life cruising around with Josh, a man three years older than her. The freedom Josh offered her was magnetic.

When things were good between them, they were amazing. When things got tense, it was volcanic. Josh had smashed a mirror, ripped a seatbelt from his car, and fought other tough guys in the pub. After every outburst, Beth brought him back down. His anchor. She could handle his ugliness beautifully.

'How is whatever is going on here my fault?' Josh is shouting.

'Because you... we... Josh, I don't remember what we were doing before I woke up in this chair,' Beth said. She starts to cry.

'We were out, I guess,' Josh replies.

'Out where? Where were we before? Where are we now?' Beth says as tears stream and her nose bubbles.

'Look, I don't know. We'll figure it out. Together.' Josh wasn't reassuring her. He was barely reassuring himself.

He stands by the cart for a moment and looks around. His mind, like this place, goes blank. How are they going to get out of this? Josh slumps down the side of the rollercoaster seat. He thuds his head repeatedly off the cart. Beth's head is in her hands and she keeps sobbing. They continue this way for an immeasurable amount of time.

'Wait a minute, I have an idea,' Josh says. He moves off, as fast as someone in this place can. It still feels as though the place is stopping him from going faster than a slow stroll.

Beth calls his name.

He ignores her; he's only a few feet away.

Josh is at the nearest of the strange wooden blocks. Despite it being larger than the average children's plaything, it shouldn't have been enough to trip him up. That means it has weight to it so it could be used to smash the restraints on Beth's rollercoaster cart. Josh's hand wraps around the blue block with a pudgy cartoon elephant on it. He pulls with all his strength. He can't lift the block. It looks like wood, that much he can see, but the texture feels different. It's harder. It's rougher. It's heavier.

'Come on, please,' he pants. His teeth grind as he tugs.

'Josh! Come back, please,' Beth pleads.

Josh obeys, dragging his heels begrudgingly.

'Where did you go?' Beth asks, reaching out to him.

'I was right over there,' Josh says, gesturing toward the blue block.

'I couldn't see you,' Beth says. 'You disappeared.'

At first, all Josh could see was the strange liquid on the ground. Nothing more. He wasn't trapped in some ridiculous theme-park ride. As he'd wandered around, more of this place became clear to him. Beth didn't have that same luxury.

Josh scratches his head again. The wetness is unbearable. Like an itch just out of reach. He holds her hands and kisses them both, saying, 'I promise I won't go anywhere again, baby. I'll be right here. We'll figure out how to get this thing off you.'

She pauses for a moment, looking in his eyes. There's a hint of sadness on her face, as if she's realised something. She says, 'I don't think you'll get me out of this one.'

'Course I will,' he replies with a wink.

'You're the reason we're in this mess,' Beth snaps.

Josh steps back, dropping Beth's hands

She can still see him. He hasn't vanished into the abyss again. She sees his whole face drop and his posture slump. He's realised what happened. He's defeated. He's sorry.

'I don't know where we are,' Beth says, 'but I remember how we got here. It was fuzzy, like this place. But I remember now.'

'Me too,' Josh says. 'I'm so sorry, Beth. I did this to us.'

Beth goes to embrace Josh as well as she can from her

restrictive seating. But she stops. Instead, she points. She points at something behind Josh and screams. Josh spins, seeing what she's pointing at. He curses and stumbles backwards, tripping over another of the wooden weights.

THEIR SCREAMS ARE HARDLY JUSTIFIED. *What's so scary about little old me?*

I always hate this part. I do a nice thing and they judge me based on my appearance. They point and scream and cry and run. Well, they try to run. I don't let them get far.

Beth writhes in her chair. The rollercoaster seat was a nice touch, I must admit. Added to the child-friendly atmosphere of the place. A foil balloon, fun blocks to play with, I've outdone myself this time. Really eased them into this situation.

Josh is a broken record. He can't lift the restraint from Beth's body, he can't touch the liquid, and he can't pick up the blocks. Yet here he is again, trying to pick up the nearest colourful wooden object to hurl at me. As before, he fails. He crawls to Beth once more and grabs her hand.

I clear my throat. I wonder how that sounds to mortal ears.

I speak, as concisely as I can. 'You remember what happened. That's why you're here. Without that, you'd be living here normally. Remembrance is the death of life.'

They stare at me blankly. The fear, the fight, has gone from their eyes. They seem resigned to what's coming next. I gave them a chance to stay here. But they had to remember. They always remember. One of these days, someone won't. They'll choose to stay with me instead. It's better than the alternative, surely.

'Positions, please,' I say.

Beth goes limp, her head slumping off the balloon, as it had been before. She tries to resist and lift her head up. Her tears are flooding.

Josh moves back to the still-expanding pool of liquid that he'd woken up in. He lies down, his head positioned exactly where it had been before.

This is just the way it has to be. I don't like forcing them. But this is my domain. They have to do what I say. They could have stayed here forever. If only they hadn't remembered.

'Beth,' Josh shouts, 'I'm so sorry. I never meant for this to happen.'

'I know,' Beth replies, 'I know.'

'You two are cute,' I say, 'but it's time to return to our scheduled programming.'

Their resistance stops. Josh falls straight back to sleep in the puddle, and Beth is unconscious with her head against the foil balloon.

I take a final look around. I really tried with this one. There's only so much you can do with a scene as gruesome as this one. Perhaps a child-friendly illusion isn't the way to go.

The emptiness fades, and I fade with it. I am only visible in the emptiness.

The scene returns to what it always had been.

Beth's rollercoaster chair transforms back into a car. Her head is no longer lying limp against a balloon but instead rests against the puffy airbag of the passenger seat. Blood pours from her head and pools on the mat beneath her feet.

The front of the car is completely wrecked. It impacted a brick wall at fifty-seven miles per hour. Without a seatbelt in the driver's side, Josh was launched from the vehicle. He landed on concrete. He died instantly. Blood erupted from his head. I can see it now, the redness stuck to his scalp. No wonder the wetness bugged him so much.

I designed the various bricks of the wall that the car dislodged on impact as colourful wooden blocks instead, trying to ease Josh into a nostalgic calmness. It was all for them.

Time begins again. I managed to snag Beth and Josh in their final moment. The last second between being alive and being dead. I tried to give them an alternative to death. They chose to remember instead. Why would you ever choose to remember you were dead? If they'd just embraced the life I'd given them, we all could have lived here. Together.

I can't let myself get worked up about it. There's always more people. More victims. More friends. On to the next.

13

THE HAUNTED FOREST

ROBIN BARKER

It was on the edge of Cluj, Romania's second city that they found it.

Hoia-Baciu.

The haunted forest.

Their coach pulled up and they got out. Craig and Luke joined a line of other tourists opposite the first line of trees. An atmosphere of nervous energy filled the air around them. It was their first trip since leaving university in England and they really wanted it to be special. A trip to Eastern Europe and Hoia-Baciu was Craig's brainchild.

'It'll certainly be memorable,' he told his friend.

Only after several hours and a few rounds of tequila did they finally reach agreement. Luke wasn't really taken with the idea, but Craig managed to convince him. A trip to the haunted land of Count Dracula. Now, standing on the edge of the forest, Craig felt doubts creeping in. Nerves too.

Is this the best idea I've ever had... or the worst?

Craig glanced at his watch. It was evening in Romania. Soon it would be dark. Their tour guide smiled.

'Not having second thoughts, are you?' he asked in clipped tones.

Craig shook his head.

'Are you sure? It's not too late to turn back.'

'He's sure,' Luke said. 'Aren't you, buddy?'

Craig's expression failed to fill the tour guide with much confidence, but after some cajoling, he shrugged his shoulders. It wasn't just the haunted tour, which made him nervous, but the guide's pale complexion. It didn't seem right. He had had a nightmare about vampires on the plane journey. The forest didn't make him feel much better. Darkness oozed from it, reaching out for him with thin, black tendrils. No one else seemed to notice this.

The guide cleared his throat.

'Welcome to Hoia-Baciu Forest,' he said. 'My name is Constantin and I will be your guide for our little tour. Before I begin, are there any questions?'

'I've got one,' Craig replied. 'Do...'

'Vampires exist?' Constantin said, interrupting him.

'Yeah.'

When in Transylvania...

'If I was to tell you that I'm a direct descendant of Vlad Dracul, would you believe me?'

The two tourists looked at each other. For a few seconds they were silent, but then they fell about laughing. It was a joke. Vampires weren't real. Something about Constantin's expression, though, suggested it wasn't meant to be funny. It was almost as if he believed it was true.

'So,' Constantin continued, 'now we've cleared that up, I will tell you what we're here for. White sheets and things that go bump in the night. You are familiar with these?'

Luke grimaced.

'I don't believe in ghosts,' he muttered. 'The only reason I came along was to see the look on his face when we find *nothing*,' he added, indicating Craig beside him.

'A non-believer,' Constantin murmured. 'Let's see if we can convert you, no?'

Luke snorted derisively.

Craig felt the darkness of the forest reaching out for him again, only this time it had a voice. *Come in,* it said. *We won't bite.* He couldn't place it, but it wasn't human. Craig felt goosebumps on his arm, but he rolled down his shirtsleeves in a bid to try and disguise his discomfort. It failed.

Constantin, ever observant, noticed.

'Cold?' he asked.

Craig shook his head.

'Christ's sake, mate, it's like a hundred degrees out here,' said Luke.

'It's nothing,' Craig replied. Then, by way of distraction, he added, 'What does Hoia-Baciu stand for anyway?'

'A good question,' Constantin replied. 'One I will answer when we have made our way into the forest. Are you ready?'

Craig slung his backpack over his shoulder and they walked in, Craig noting that the other tourists had went with a different guide via a separate route. Each backpack had enough food and water to last the night. There were no cafés or convenience stores in Hoia-Baciu Forest.

'This place was named after a shepherd who went missing along with two hundred of his flock,' Constantin remarked. 'You won't find many locals near here for fear of not returning. I, myself, am from Bucharest, over four hundred kilometres away, so I'm not worried. If I disappear it might be a blessing in disguise, because then I won't have to pay alimony anymore...'

This elicited more laughs from the two men.

'Hoia-Baciu is known as the haunted forest,' Constantin continued, 'which is why you are here. Do you know what happened in 1968 to bring it to people's attention?'

They shook their heads.

'You know UFOs...?'

'Unidentified flying objects,' Craig replied.

Constantin nodded.

'A photographer claimed he had a picture of a UFO hovering over the clearing I'll be showing you tonight. Can you believe it?'

Craig had read up on the clearing online before they'd arrived. It was an oval in which nothing grew. Nothing ever would. He touched one of the trees and was surprised by how cold it felt. Lifeless almost. It was made even weirder still by the fact that a gloom descended on them as they made their way deeper into the forest. The tree cover was thick, hardly letting any natural light inside. Craig glanced back at Luke, but he couldn't see him. Apart from Constantin he was alone.

Where was he?

His heart pounded. He turned and Luke jumped out at him. It gave Craig a hell of a shock.

'You should see your face,' Luke proclaimed.

'Like I've seen a ghost?' Craig asked.

'I'm afraid that doesn't count as a paranormal encounter,' Constantin remarked. 'For those, we must keep on going.'

All light was choked from overhead as night fell. The canopy of trees was no longer a refreshing break from the heat of the day. It was restrictive and unsettling. Constantin turned on his torch, lighting their way. They did the same. Craig shone his at a nearby tree, which was twisted beyond recognition. He took a photo on his mobile phone. It said "no service" in a corner of the screen.

'Have you got any signal, Luke?' he asked.

His friend shook his head. If there were any problems no one could call out. Constantin seemed amused by this. Craig wondered if they'd made the right choice picking him as their guide. His tour company had seemed shady at best. It was cheap, but was that always the best option? His mood wasn't helped when Luke startled him by calling out.

'Hey, who's there?'

Craig tried to see what his friend was looking at, but he couldn't at first. Then he saw a man in a white robe. Craig's initial nervousness had now given way to fright. He turned to his friend and then looked back, but the man was gone.

Ghost-like.

'Was that a...?' Luke started to say.

Constantin nodded. It was an almost imperceptible movement.

'Of course,' he replied. 'This is a haunted tour. Do we have a believer now?'

'No,' Luke replied, 'that was a man. As real as you and me. I'm going to go and check it out.'

Luke took off. Craig was about to follow him when he felt a cold hand on his arm. Constantin was standing next to him, his grip vice-like.

'Let him go,' he replied. 'If you go after him you might get lost. As your guide I have to make sure you get back in one piece.'

'What about him?' Craig asked.

'He'll be back in a minute. We'll take a break.'

Craig turned and looked back the way his friend had gone. The sound of his footsteps receded, but his torchlight continued to twinkle in the darkness. The longer he saw that the better he felt. It meant he was okay. Craig took the opportunity to rest while he could. He lit up a cigarette while he waited for Luke to return.

'You know those things will kill you,' Constantin remarked. 'But they're not the only things in this world that will.'

Craig frowned. Something was off about what he'd just said. Constantin might have said the "world", but he meant right there. It made him think. Bears, snakes, spiders, wolves, wild cats even. The one creature in this wood Craig didn't want to think about were the bats, which were famed in Romania. Luke didn't believe in ghosts and there was no way he believed in vampires either.

'Don't you think Luke's been gone a long time?' he said.

His torchlight was still visible. Craig knew he should have been satisfied with this, but he wasn't. It wasn't moving anymore.

'I'm going to look for him,' Craig continued.

'I said he will be back in a minute,' Constantin replied.

Craig frowned. He didn't want to get into an argument about

the fact that the minute was over already. It was childish at best. So, he ran off before their guide could stop him. He sprinted toward the torchlight. Loose twigs cracked beneath his feet. It wasn't the quietest he'd ever been, but then he wasn't trying to be. He called out Luke's name, but there was no response. He found his torch nestled against the exposed roots of a tree, but he was nowhere to be seen. Feeling a presence behind him, he turned and found Constantin standing there. Craig hadn't heard cracking or any sound whatsoever. His silence was unnerving.

'He's not here,' Craig exclaimed.

Constantin shrugged his shoulders and then turned away. Craig couldn't believe he was giving up.

'Where are you going?' he asked. 'We can't just leave him here.'

'He knows we're heading to the clearing,' Constantin replied, 'so, I suggest we make our way and he can meet us there.'

'Good idea,' Craig said, before raising his voice. 'Meet us in the clearing, Luke.'

He hoped his friend would hear. Constantin bent down to pick up the torch, but he stopped him. Luke would need it to find his way. The guide shrugged again and shuffled off. Craig struggled to keep pace with him. They made progress and were soon back on the right path.

'Don't worry,' Constantin said. 'He will find his way to the clearing and us. It's not too far to go now. We can wait for him there.'

I'm glad you have faith in that.

Craig tried to shake the feeling that they'd never see him again and followed Constantin further into the forest. Gnarled trees and strange foliage were not enough to catch his attention. He was worried about Luke. His focus was on getting to the clearing and, hopefully, finding his friend.

According to the internet the clearing was the creepiest part of Hoia-Baciu Forest. It defied soil scientists who were unable to explain why nothing would grow there. Craig cared little for these stories. The fact was that Luke was missing. He called his friend's name, but there was no response.

'Where is he?' Craig asked.

'He'll be here soon,' Constantin replied.

'How do you know? He went off in search of that strange man...'

Craig couldn't bring himself to call him a ghost.

'And we haven't seen him since. What if he's lost or worse?'

Constantin remained neutral. Craig wondered what it would take for him to show any sort of emotion.

'I could go and look for him,' he said, 'if that would make you feel any better.'

Craig shook his head.

'You can't leave me here,' he said.

A rustle in the undergrowth nearby made him jump. Craig fixed the spot with a stare.

Constantin laughed. 'Here he is now.'

'Luke, is that you?' Craig yelled.

There was no response. The rustling had stopped. Craig tried several more times, but with no luck.

'Why isn't he replying?'

'It could be an animal,' Constantin replied, unconvincingly. 'Maybe you scared it with your voice.'

Craig disagreed. It was his friend, finally returned to him. He held on to that hope as he ran forward into the undergrowth. The rustling started up again. Then there was a scream. Craig backed slowly out of the undergrowth. His hands were raised slightly in front of him, a submissive gesture. He was being followed out by the white-robed figure they'd seen earlier. There was something almost regal about him. Craig shone his torch.

Luke.

Craig's friend was limp in the man's arms. When the man let go of him, he slumped lifelessly to the ground. Blood trickled from two little puncture wounds on his neck.

Craig was about to rush to his friend's aid when he felt the guide's hands on him. That same devilish grip. His earlier feeling had been right. If only he'd spoken out.

'What the hell is this?' Craig asked.

'I'm sorry if you felt you were deceived,' Constantin replied. The guide bared his elongated teeth.

'Are you a… vampire?' Craig replied. 'But… how is that possible? You were out in daylight.'

Constantin sighed. 'A common misconception,' he replied. 'We are nocturnal dwellers, yes, but light isn't as bad for us as you might imagine.'

Craig tried to wriggle free, but he was unable to. Others began appearing out of the dark forest. Men, women, children even. He wondered if he might be able to appeal to them for help, but then, chillingly, he realised they were all vampires.

Ghosts, but with fangs.

'Unfortunately, history and your people have not been so kind to us,' Constantin continued. 'We now find ourselves banished to Hoia-Baciu Forest. If people discover what we're doing here we will be wiped out. There was no other way we could get you here, but under the pretence of a haunted tour. We, too, must feed, you see.'

Craig felt physically sick. Luke had not moved at all. Blood was no longer flowing from the wounds on his neck, which wasn't a good sign. It meant his heart had stopped. He was dead.

Craig tried to shake himself free of Constantin's hold, but it was far too difficult. It was as if he was a wildebeest trying to free himself from the jaws of a crocodile. Constantin leant forward and Craig felt sharp teeth grazing his neck. There was no way he was going to let them turn him. Not like his friend. As Constantin leant in further, Craig felt his grip loosen.

This is my moment.

Craig shoved back against him and managed to free himself. He stumbled around, trying to find an escape route and to avoid Luke's dead eyes at the same time.

I'm sorry. I'm so, so sorry.

Constantin smiled, enjoying the sight of Craig's panic.

The white-robed vampire bristled with barely restrained anger.

'Stop him!' he bellowed.

Craig felt trapped. The circle was closing in on him, but then he sensed an opportunity – the smallest of gaps between two of the children – but it was his only chance. So, he turned and fled in their direction. He pushed them out of the way and hurried toward the relative protection of the nearby treeline.

'Don't worry,' Constantin said, 'he won't get far. And we do have another lot coming in soon.'

What does he mean?

Craig gave it no more thought. He crashed through the forest. Eventually arriving at the same spot they'd stopped to take a rest, he saw Luke's torch and was suddenly rejuvenated. Some time later, although it felt like a lifetime, he reached the edge of the forest. Their transport was still there by the side of the road and next to it was another coach.

It was filled with tourists.

They were innocents unaware of the mortal danger they would soon find themselves in. They thought they were there to see ghosts, but they were being led to their deaths. Craig considered warning them, but when two guides got out of the front of the truck he held back. They were as pale as Constantin, who now also came into view. Constantin looked around, but his quarry was out of sight. Craig watched the tourists being led into Hoia-Baciu Forest with a sense of dread.

He waited for them to disappear and then he took off down the dirt track they'd driven along earlier. He remembered passing houses on the way. He ran to the nearest one and banged on the front door. After a few seconds it opened and an old woman answered.

'Please, can you help me!' Craig exclaimed.

The woman eyed him coldly. She didn't understand him.

'Do you speak English?' he asked. 'Does anyone here speak English?'

'I do...'

A young man stepped forward. The old lady vanished back into the house.

'What is the matter?' he asked.

'Vampires attacked my friends. We must call the police.'

'*Politie*, of course,' the young man replied. 'Come in, you can use our telephone.'

Craig accepted the invitation. The front door closed behind him and he was relieved to finally be away from Hoia-Baciu Forest. What he failed to acknowledge, however, was the lack of surprise when he mentioned vampires. Craig also didn't notice how pale his host was. There was no telephone, there would be no call. The family had no business with the police nor did they fear vampires. For they were one and the same.

14

THE SIREN TREE

CHRIS JAMES

In his treatise on *Dangerous Plants of the World* (1587), Amalfus Lodge referred briefly to the mythical Siren Tree, also known as the Hunting Tree or the Angel Tree. The brevity of his entry points to both his scepticism and the paucity of known fact.

According to Lodge, a single reference to the tree was recorded in the field notes of the Ni-Land botanist and scholar Tai-Tac. Moreover, had it not been for the academic stature of Tai-Tac within the university and his contribution in general to botanic academia, it is doubtful that it would have been referenced at all.

The translation from Tai-Tac's personal notes states: *Siren Tree; dangerous predatory chimaera. Approach only with fire. Ten leagues is too close to this abomination.*

MOUNTAINOUS THUNDERCLOUDS GATHERED OVERHEAD. It was late November, and more than a hint of winter was in the air. Skittish flurries became protracted blows, shaking the boughs of trees and causing the fallen leaves to dance in swirling eddies. All over the forest, creatures fled homeward. One of the last dragonflies of the year made a low-level pass over the field, unable to fly higher in the plummeting air pressure. It was not a good time to be abroad unless you had no choice.

Felix had no choice. He had to get his master's sheep home from the market in Church-Bailie to the farm in Wood-Bailie; a distance of two leagues or more across the forest. Even with the help of the old dog, Mr Peeps, it would take two or more hours.

Felix looked forward to market days. Today was no exception. The early part of the day had been bathed in late-autumn sun, and new cider flowed. Whilst his master, Joseph, had haggled, sold and bought a new ram and other stock, Felix had renewed his acquaintance with the local brew and the other farm boys. Much discussion was held over the quality of the cider and if it was as good as last year's. The more they drank, the more they agreed it was likely a vintage year, a year of legend.

Market days were also a chance to meet with the local girls and to catch up on local gossip. Not unusually, a fight had broken out. Bill Medley had drunkenly tried to kiss little Betty Long. Betty's father, a short, wiry man with a quick temper, had taken exception to this and had grabbed Bill by the collar and thrown him to the ground. Although Bill was four sheets to the wind, he was still twice the size of Midge Long, Betty's da. Before the older men got involved, Midge had already taken a beating. Nursing a bleeding nose, Midge sat on an upturned keg while Betty wiped the blood away, occasionally casting angry glances at the drunken youths.

Felix helped Midge to his feet just as Bill's father, Jack Medley, arrived. A big man, Jack, not known to suffer fools gladly, least of all Bill, of whom he expected more. Red-faced and shouting, Jack slapped Bill so hard across the face that he fell backwards into the water trough. While everyone else laughed, Bill struggled to hold back his tears. He stared at his feet and muttered, 'Sorry, Da.' After all was said and done, apologies were whimpered and arrangements were made; Bill would work the next four Sundays for Midge without pay. The silver lining was that he would also get to see Betty, which almost made up for his public humiliation.

With everything happening, Felix didn't realise how late it had gotten. Joseph had left two hours earlier on his pony, insisting that Felix should follow right away with the livestock. Later than expected but feeling a cheerful glow, Felix hurried toward the forest path, turning up his collar against the chill weather. Progress was slow as the sheep tried to keep as far away from the dog as possible. Eventually, the remnants of the canopy closed overhead.

Felix always felt that the beech trees, with their smooth grey bark, resembled the legs of giant animals marching beside him. This impression was intensified by their swaying and lurching as wind and rain tore through their upper branches. After an hour of trudging along the muddy, rutted path, daylight faded into gloom. More than once, Felix felt an eerie sensation that he was being watched but dismissed it as a trick of his imagination.

His waxed cotton overcoat was heavy but could be relied on to keep him mostly dry. The neck, however, was loose and did little to protect him from the heavy drips from above. With water trickling down his neck, Felix kept his head down and tramped onward. Before long, his mind turned to more pleasant things. In his reverie, he failed to notice he had left the path. A bramble snagged his leg, causing him to return to the present.

Through the howling wind, he fancied he all but heard a girl singing.

THE STORM HAD RAGED all night. By morning, there was a welcome break in the weather. Patches of blue sky intermingled with thin wispy clouds strung across the sky. Joseph was puzzled that the sheep were not shut in the pen, but was relieved they were herded into a corner of the farmyard under the watchful gaze of Mr Peeps. Sheep left unpenned tended to wander off. Unattended, they could be hurt, hunted, stolen, drowned or end up bloated through grazing on legumes like clover. Of all the farm animals Joseph knew, sheep were the most stupid; almost born to die.

With his shepherd's crook and Mr Peeps helping, Joseph quickly herded the sheep to the pens and shut them in. Angrily, he stomped to the hut where Felix slept and banged loudly on the door. No answer. Banging again, he expected to hear the boy tumble to the door looking worse for wear, but remorseful.

Pushing the door open, it was clear the cot hadn't been slept on. Equally strange was Mr Peeps's behaviour. The dog kept whining and running to the gate. *Odd,* Joseph thought. *Where on earth has that boy got to?*

Not being a man to act rashly or without due consideration, Joseph sat a while on the stout stone wall surrounding the well and lit the remaining tobacco flakes in his clay pipe. His first thought was that Felix was probably recovering from an excess of cider under a bush nearby, but that didn't seem in character. Frowning deeply, he fetched his pony from the stable and set off back down the forest path, calling Mr Peeps to heel as he went.

Thirty minutes later, Mr Peeps stopped dead in the path and started barking. 'Quiet, boy,' Joseph said. Mr Peeps slunk away behind the pony with his tail between his legs. The forest, usually a noisy place full of calling birds and chattering animals, was eerily silent. Joseph turned his head to one side. He could have sworn he heard a small voice call him.

Pulling on the reins of his pony, he turned to face the direction from which the sound had come. Nothing appeared out of place. A deep sense of unease came over him. The hairs on the back of his neck stood up. He felt more than being watched, he felt hunted. The ground shuddered as something heavy moved. The fetid stench of rotting meat drifted to where he sat.

His pony trembled beneath him, wide-eyed and nostrils flaring. Backing away, Joseph fought to get him under control. Mr Peeps, ears flat against his head, was bravely barking at something Joseph couldn't see. Looking back over his shoulder Joseph suddenly froze. About thirty paces away, on the path he had just travelled, stood a tree-like creature. Its bark was silver-grey and appeared soft and sinewy, resembling the skin of a snake. It was mesmerising in its beauty, with a ring of motile branches emerging symmetrically from a central point. Each branch ended in several barbed tips that dripped a dark-green ichor. On one branch, shreds of a waxed cotton overcoat hung loosely.

Despite his overwhelming fear and desire to run, Joseph felt an intense desire to move closer. Mr Peeps barked again, interrupting his thoughts. In the brief moment it took for Joseph to look toward the dog, the tree had vanished.

Frantically, Joseph turned around, searching for where it had gone. Mr Peeps growled, looking upward. Descending rapidly through the canopy toward Joseph was a silver form. Wicked prongs of poison swept toward him. The pony suddenly reared and bolted. Behind him, he heard a high-pitched scream and the sound of something heavy hitting the ground. The terrified pony sped down the forest path at breakneck speed, Joseph desperately clinging to the saddle.

Approaching the forest edge, the pony went under a low-hanging branch, tearing Joseph from his seat. Landing heavily, Joseph quickly picked himself up. The oppressive silence settled around him like a heavy drape. A little away off, deeper in the forest, he could hear the sound of axes rhythmically cutting wood. Collecting his hat, he ran toward the sound.

Cut trees lay strewn about a clearing. Men in shirtsleeves laboured to strip off the branches, while others gathered around a brush fire, smoking long clay pipes, their seven-pound felling axes leaning against a tree. Jack Medley stood in their midst, a good head and shoulders above the others. He was pointing to a stand of young oak trees he wanted left as an uncut copse. Out of breath and panting, Joseph staggered into the clearing. Jack turned toward the unusual arrival. 'Morning, Jo,' said Jack, looking quizzically at the farmer. 'You look like a man with a problem? Seems you also lost your pony.'

'More than that,' Joseph replied, 'there's some damn beast loose in the forest. It would have got me, but for the dog and the pony bolting. I fear it's taken poor Felix.'

'A beast, you say? What sort of a beast?' said Jack. 'Me and the boys have been here since sunrise, and we've not heard or seen a thing, let alone a beast. What does this beast look like, Jo?'

Joseph described it as a silver tree-like creature with snaking branches that dripped a green poison and soundlessly called to him. Sceptically, Jack raised an eyebrow and turned to the men asking if they had seen anything strange. Old Corrie Miller, a man well past his prime, put his hand up and spoke. 'Been a bit quiet, Jack, but nothing out of the ordinary. I couldn't hear much else with you and the lads cutting and shouting. Maybe young Bill has heard something? Ears on him like a bat, that boy. I'll go down and check on him. He's supposed to be clearing gorse down by the Old Mill, but I reckon he's sleeping off the cider from yesterday, or the lovesickness has taken him.' Chuckling at his own wit, Corrie ambled down the hill toward the Old Mill.

BILL WOKE to a blue sky and the silence of the forest. More than anything, it was the silence that had stirred him from his sleep. Sitting up, Bill looked around uneasily. Something was off, but nothing he could put his finger on, just the silence, a palpable pause in the continuity of life. The only noise came from the millstream gushing and burbling through the narrow gulley where the mill-wheel once had stood. Through the near silence, a small voice called him over the sound of the stream. It sounded a bit like Betty, but why, he thought, would Betty be here in the forest, unless, of course, she had come to forgive him for his drunken behaviour the day before? To his left, he caught a glimpse of something moving so fast he could barely track it. Tall, shining and beautiful, it came to a stop, gracefully settling on the opposite bank of the stream. It was easily the loveliest thing he had ever seen. It called to him and he yearned to be near it. It made no attempt to cross the stream. Bill, entranced, walked to the edge of the stream and reached out with his hand. Faster than the speed of thought, a branch whipped out, the tip catching his fingers. Bill pulled it back quickly as a paralysing numbness started to spread up his arm.

Bill cursed, holding his hand to his chest and looked at a now empty space where the tree had stood. Downstream, it seemed as if a silver light played up and down the bank seeking a crossing point.

'BILL, you lazy cur, where are you?' Corrie emerged from a stand of dying bracken and looked across the valley bottom. To the right of the Old Mill, he saw Bill running uphill toward him, carrying his right arm as if in a sling. Bill, gasping, shouted, 'Corrie, run!' An odd movement flared along the bank of the stream, behind the boy, moving unnaturally quickly toward the Roman bridge.

Fear was etched into the boy's face as he stumbled into Corrie, nearly knocking him over. 'Corrie, don't ask! Just get me back to Da. Da, it got me!' Bill shouted as he and Corrie staggered out of breath into the clearing.

'Bill? What's got you?' asked Jack as he strode over to his son.

Holding his arm out, Bill showed a puncture mark in his right hand. 'Da, it's gone numb and I can't move my fingers.'

'Son, look at me, and tell me slowly, what did this to you?'

Bill recounted his waking by the Old Mill, to the Angel Tree that called to him and then stung him. Corrie confirmed that there really was something dangerous in the forest and that whatever it was, it couldn't just cross the stream and was, so far as he could see, moving fast downstream.

Jack nodded, his mind working quickly, adding to what Joseph had already described. He had worked out that by now the beast would have reached the Roman bridge and would shortly be heading in their direction from the west.

'Pile brush in the centre of the clearing and set it on fire,' Jack ordered. In minutes, ten men had built and set a raging fire. He told the men to pick up their axes and form a line with their backs to the flames. Jack took his place in the middle of the line.

Barking, Mr Peeps ran into the clearing, turning again to snarl at an invisible foe before running to stand by Joseph.

The sun slipped behind a cloud, casting shade over the clearing. In contrast, an unearthly light appeared on the far side. One of the men dropped his axe and began to walk toward it, smiling as if to greet an old friend. Jack shouted too late as a branch snaked out, piercing the man and lifting him effortlessly from his feet toward the central gap in the circle of branches.

With its branch now turned inwards to feed, Jack ran forward, swinging his axe in a mighty blow at the centre of the creature. It connected and dug deep, green ichor flowed from a wound. A mental scream rang through Jack's mind, causing him to leave his axe-head buried in the trunk. Several men dropped their axes, holding their hands to their heads in pain. Through the screaming, Jack picked up a flaming branch and advanced on the creature, which retreated before the blazing prong. Swinging the burning branch round his head, Jack released it, sending it soaring up toward the central point between the branches. Rebounding off one of the limbs, it dropped directly into the central maw, sending a plume of green flame skywards.

Slowly, the mental screaming faded. The entire creature folded in on itself, getting smaller and smaller. Finally, all that remained was a round, flat disc that spun on its axis before settling. In minutes, it had swelled to four times its size before bursting with a crack to release a cloud of green spores, which slowly dissipated on the breeze.

Joseph knelt by the fire, examining the wound in Bill's hand

and thinking back to his youth when his da had limped home with a similar wound in his leg. He didn't speak much about it, but told him to fetch Ma Long, the wise woman. She had set a tub of water so hot it scalded. Joseph remembered his scream of pain as his leg was immersed. For days after, he remembered his da could barely walk. He had to do much of the work in his place. After what seemed like an age, the blistering faded along with the green tinge, and the leg healed.

Later that evening, Bill screamed soundlessly as his arm was immersed in near-boiling water. Betty bound his wound as she had been taught by her grandmother. In truth, she was inwardly sorry that Bill would not be, after all, visiting every Sunday for the next four weeks. Or at least until his arm got better.

Epilogue

Of Felix, everyone had been very sad at his passing. A regrettable accident. Such a nice lad. A veil was drawn over all else. Folks were, after all, very superstitious, and Church-Bailie was a God-fearing village on a trade route through to Bath. A service was held in his memory, and an engraved stone was placed in the forest where he had fallen.

Spring was in the air. Betty was engaged to Bill, and the wedding was set for the summer. Betty was fast becoming a competent wise woman herself, just like her grandma. She had at last read every tome left to her, even the encrypted one in her grandma's own handwriting entitled, *Ni-Land for the knowing.*

In the secret garden, one of the green spores had finally germinated and was glowing softly. Smiling, Betty carefully closed the lid on the germinator, making doubly sure it was fully locked and set this time in a ring of fire. Pity, she thought, her grandma had forgotten in her old age to follow her own rules. Sadly, Betty knew she could never admit why her grandma had suddenly disappeared and her little shack had been ransacked. The few drops of green slime left on the floor were to Betty evidence enough. She remembered well one of the last things her grandmother had said to her: *Don't get old, love, some days I'd forget my own head if it weren't screwed on.*

15

THE ITALIAN PRIEST

MICHAEL HAYES

'I'm sorry, Father,' said Natalie with a smile, 'I'm afraid I don't speak Italian.'

'Ah, but *I* speak English,' replied the priest with a little twinkle in his eye.

'What was it you said to me then?' she asked.

'He is very beautiful, no?'

'Oh yes,' breathed Natalie, '*molto!*'

'So you do speak my language!' the priest said, laughing.

'Just a few words,' replied Natalie shyly.

They were in the Galleria dell'Accademia in Florence where Natalie had sat down to admire Michelangelo's *David*. Without realising it she had emitted a sigh at the sheer beauty of the statue and the priest who happened to be sitting next to her had heard her. '*Che bello*,' he had whispered thus sparking their exchange.

'*Scusi, signora*,' he continued, 'but with your dark hair and flashing eyes I thought you *were* Italian. So, English. *Va bene* – I studied at the seminary in Chatham when I was a young man. Where are you from?'

'London.'

'Ah, London. I used to visit your National Gallery back in those days. You have some of our finest work on display there. It is a good thing we Italians are not possessive,' and he gave a little chuckle.

Natalie wasn't sure if he was teasing her or not so she pointed at *David*. 'But you have kept the very best here in Florence.'

'Thank you, *signora*,' and the priest patted her hand. 'Shall we look round the gallery?' He rose slowly to his feet and took her arm. 'You don't mind?' He smiled. 'My knee is painful, but otherwise I'm not bad for my age.'

This was true. Natalie guessed he was in his sixties but with his square jaw and straight back he looked more like a distinguished Continental film star than a priest – Yves Montand perhaps or Marcello Mastroianni. Natalie was happy to take his arm.

He was a very good guide, something of an art expert in fact, and Natalie was glad to be in his company. She particularly liked Michelangelo's *Slaves*; unfinished statues, with the figures just beginning to emerge from the marble from which they were carved.

'Oh,' she exclaimed, 'I wish they would simply shake themselves and step free.'

'Like a dog after a swim,' agreed the priest.

They stayed in the gallery until late afternoon when the priest suggested that they should go and have a little drink together. 'But do not tell my abbot,' he said with a wink. 'He would be outraged that a sixty-five-year-old priest should consort with a beautiful woman such as you. Jealousy is a terrible thing,' and with a laugh he gave her hand another pat.

'I'd love to,' agreed Natalie, flattered. 'But don't you have to say Mass or attend Evensong or something?'

The priest shook his head and smiled ruefully.

'Alas,' he said, 'the people of Florence, like people everywhere, no longer have need for God in their lives. Where we used to celebrate two Masses a day now there is only one – and the congregations become smaller all the time. It is very sad.'

'So which is your church?' asked Natalie.

'I serve the Dominican Order,' replied the priest, 'and I divide my time between San Marco in the piazza outside the gallery here and Santa Maria Novella to the west. Come, before the rain gets any worse.'

It was early winter and already dark as they left the gallery.

'I thought the sun always shone in Italy,' said Natalie with a laugh. She hugged the priest's arm as he put up his umbrella and they hurried into a nearby café-bar.

'*Buona sera, Padre*,' said la signora behind the counter. '*Fa brutto ancora!*'

'Yes,' agreed the priest, 'the weather's terrible again!'

La signora obviously knew the priest because she came straight to his table with a bottle and two glasses. He poured the drinks and raised his glass.

'But where are my manners? We haven't introduced ourselves! I am Francesco di Giorgio,' he exclaimed.

'And I am Natalie Payne, *piacere!*'

'Ha!' exclaimed the priest, 'you *do* speak my language. *Piacere* – pleasure to meet you! So, what are you doing in my beautiful, if rather wet city?'

A look of sadness crossed Natalie's face. 'I recently lost my husband. We were married on the 4th of November 1986 so the day after tomorrow would have been our twentieth wedding anniversary – I just wanted to get away for a while, so it wouldn't hurt so much. Besides,' she said, forcing herself to become cheerful again, 'I'm doing an art course and what better place to study art than Florence?'

'Exactly!' agreed the priest. He offered his condolences for her loss then was silent for a moment. 'We, the people of Florence, also suffer an unwanted anniversary in two days' time,' and he, too, looked sad for a moment. 'But let us think of the present! If you would like a guide, I know something of the art of Florence and humbly offer my services – on one condition!'

'And what's that?' said Natalie with a smile.

'That you have dinner with me!'

That night, as she lay in her hotel bed, Natalie couldn't help but feel a little amazed at herself: not only had she gone to dinner with the priest but she had also become a little tipsy with wine and found herself enjoying his company very much – it had been *fun*. Knowing he was a priest had allowed her to relax and let her guard down; there was no threat from a man of the cloth, no fear of complications; she had felt safe.

Furthermore, Father Francesco's knowledge of Renaissance Art was profound and she knew immediately that he could help enormously with her studies. To that end he had promised to show her round San Marco the next morning and Santa Maria Novella in the afternoon.

She felt a sudden flicker of guilt. George, her husband, had only been gone for eight months – what would *he* think?

'I've never been religious – he'd probably laugh at the irony,' she said softly as she drifted off to sleep.

The next day she was up with the lark.

Why does breakfast coffee in Italy taste so much nicer than anywhere else? she wondered as she helped herself to a second cup. She was reading about the church of San Marco in her guide book: the frescoes by Fra Angelico were not to be missed.

She had agreed to meet Father Francesco at eleven. Braving the rain which still persisted, Natalie went out early to explore and take in the atmosphere of the city.

Shortly before eleven she arrived at the same café as the previous night.

'*Buongiorno, signora, piove ancora!*' said the proprietress, rolling her eyes.

Natalie realised that she meant "it's still raining!" and smiled. She ordered a *panino* and a coffee and took out her guide book. She sat reading for a while and glanced at her watch: quarter past; no sign of the priest. She finished her coffee and read a bit more. Half past. Still no sign of Father Francesco. She ordered another coffee.

Noon came and went and the priest still had not arrived. Natalie paid her bill and walked over to the church. It was locked. A sign said it was open for visitors from 2pm – 5pm.

She was standing wondering what to do when the door opened and an old woman, probably a cleaner, came out.

'Excuse me, signora,' said Natalie, 'is Father Francesco there?'

The old woman looked blank.

'Father Francesco di Giorgio – *il Padre*,' pressed Natalie.

'*Lui non è qui*,' said the old woman, shaking her head.

'But I was supposed to meet him,' protested Natalie.

The old woman shook her head once more and shrugged her shoulders.

Just then the door opened again and a young priest came out.

'Can I help you, *signora*?' he asked.

'Oh, thank you! I feel so foolish not speaking Italian. I have an appointment with Father Francesco – can you tell him I'm here?'

'I'm sorry, *signora*, there is some mistake. There is no Father Francesco here at San Marco.'

'But he said he'd show me the frescoes – Father Francesco di Giorgio.'

The priest smiled and shook his head. 'I'm sorry, *signora*, there is no one of that name here.'

'But... but... He was *here* – he showed me round the gallery...' Natalie tailed off lamely.

The priest was giving her a funny look. He smiled again. 'I'm sorry, *signora*. If you would like to come back later, we open for visitors at two.'

Feeling rather foolish, Natalie apologised and hurried away. She returned to her hotel room and plonked herself down in a chair. An unpleasant thought had occurred to her and she tipped the contents of her handbag onto the little desk. She opened her purse – if this Father Francesco was an imposter who was to say that he wasn't a con man too?

She sighed with relief: her money, cards and passport were all present and correct. The mysterious priest was obviously not a thief... so where had he gone?

And who was he?

Natalie's feeling of foolishness was giving way to one of indignation: how dare this man, a perfect stranger, subject her to a practical joke like this?

She decided to do a bit of detective work. She set off to Santa Maria Novella to see if anyone there knew him. When she arrived at the church, what a surprise she got – there was the priest chatting to the man in the ticket kiosk.

Natalie hurried up to him with the intention of giving him a piece of her mind but he greeted her with such genuine enthusiasm that she was taken aback. He beamed with joy and took her hand.

'I thought you weren't coming,' he said in a tone of mild reproach. 'I've been waiting for ages.'

'*You've* been waiting! Why, I've been at San Marco since eleven – just like we said,' she protested.

The priest's face fell and he put his hand to his mouth. 'San Marco? But didn't we agree to meet here at Santa Maria Novella?'

Natalie shook her head.

'Please, you must forgive me, my memory sometimes lets me down. I remember some things from years ago like yesterday – the terrible flood of 1966 for instance – but I sometimes confuse my appointments. I'm very sorry.'

Natalie's indignation vanished. She couldn't be angry with this man, he was simply too nice. Besides, he wasn't a youngster anymore and older people sometimes became a bit forgetful. But why did the cleaning lady and the young priest not know him? Surely they couldn't have forgotten too?

'My duties at San Marco are light, just a few hours a week,' explained the priest. 'The young man is new, and I am never there at the same time as the cleaner – we simply have not met. It's time,' he said, glancing at his watch, 'shall we go in?' and he led her past the ticket window where the man on duty smiled and waved her through.

'But I haven't paid,' she exclaimed.

'You are with the priest,' said the man with a shrug.

'Is Father Francesco your friend?' she asked the man.

'We never met before, but he is a priest and this is the House of God – *prego, prego!*'

And so they went in.

Any misgivings Natalie may have had about Father Francesco were soon dispelled: he was a charming companion and knew the world of art inside out.

'I could stay here all evening,' said Natalie with a sigh. 'It's so beautiful.'

'We will have to go soon, the church shuts at dusk in winter – we have already been here all afternoon,' said the priest with a smile. 'But there is one thing I must show you before it gets dark,' and he led her into the cloisters which, because of the continuing rain, were rather damp and uninviting. He pointed to a plaque high up on the wall.

'Look,' he said. 'That marks the height of the water when the Arno flooded in 1966.'

Natalie gasped. 'But it's so high!'

The priest nodded. 'Three metres.'

'And we're so far from the river.'

The priest nodded again.

'And what's that underneath the plaque?'

'A memorial to the people who died – it lists their names.'

'I didn't know,' whispered Natalie. 'And this was on the 4th of November, the same day as my anniversary?'

'Yes. 1966. The anniversary of the flood is tomorrow.'

'Oh!' exclaimed Natalie, 'I've bought tickets for a river trip to Pisa tomorrow, along the Arno to see the Leaning Tower. I was going to ask you to come.'

'Not tomorrow. There are Masses all morning and in the afternoon I would like to take you to the Basilica di San Lorenzo.'

'But I've already got the tickets,' protested Natalie.

'Pah! A few euros,' snorted the priest.

'The day after then?'

'I will be gone by then,' and the priest sadly shook his head. 'But now we are here and I want my *prosecco!*' he exclaimed. 'Come – you will have a glass of wine with me?' With a laugh he led her toward a little bar.

'Well, just the one,' said Natalie with a smile. She didn't usually drink more than a glass or two a month. 'I *am* on holiday I suppose. Where are you going by the way? I'll miss you.'

'Thank you. Some business for the Boss,' and he pointed skyward.

'The abbot?'

'You could say that,' and he gave her a mysterious smile.

The following morning, Natalie attended the memorial service in Santa Maria Novella for all those who had died in the flood. She had not been to a religious service since George's funeral and found it very moving.

Oddly, she thought, there was no sign of Father Francesco, either with the celebrants on the altar or in the congregation with the worshippers. But then again, she reasoned, the church was packed and it was very easy to miss someone. They had exchanged mobile phone numbers the previous evening to cover just such an eventuality and as she left the church she called him. But there was no need – he was outside waiting for her. He took her hands in his and kissed her cheeks.

'A beautiful service,' he said.

'*Molto,*' she agreed with a little smile.

'I said a prayer for George,' he said, giving her hand a little squeeze.

That's funny, thought Natalie. *I don't remember telling you his name.* She smiled and thanked the priest for his kindness.

'*Allora, andiamo!*' cried Father Francesco. 'I'm hungry! Let's have something to eat.'

After lunch he took her to see the Basilica di San Lorenzo where Natalie was transfixed by the Bronzino fresco of the martyrdom of Saint Lawrence, burnt to death on a griddle.

'Poor chap,' whispered the priest, crossing himself. 'It is said that he told his executioners to turn him over "because this side is done".'

When it was time to leave they had a lovely surprise: pale wintry sunshine in a sky of the clearest azure.

'It's stopped raining!' said Natalie with a laugh.

'Praise be to God,' said Father Francesco, smiling as they stepped into Piazza San Lorenzo. There was a newspaper kiosk in the piazza and as they approached it the priest quickened his step. 'Oh no,' he said, breaking into a run, 'not again!' and he snatched up a paper.

The headline read: *DISASTRO SULL'ARNO.*

'What is it? What does it say?' cried Natalie.

The priest quickly scanned the page. 'There's been a disaster on the river. All this rain has raised the water level and the captain of a pleasure boat didn't realise until too late. There wasn't room for his boat under a bridge and the upper deck was destroyed. Thirty-five dead.' He slowly lowered the paper.

Natalie put her hand on his arm. 'That was *my* boat wasn't it? The one I bought the tickets for. That should have been...'

The priest nodded and took her hand. 'You must give thanks. Go to Mass tomorrow morning at Santa Maria. I will be there also. I must go to the stricken boat now, they will need a priest.'

'Shall I come? Do you think I could do anything?'

The priest gently shook his head. 'No, *cara,* I'm afraid that not being able to speak Italian would only make things worse. But say a prayer.' And he hurried off.

'See you at Mass tomorrow,' Natalie called after him, but he didn't turn round.

It was a thoughtful and sombre Natalie who returned to the hotel that night.

Next morning, as Natalie made her way to Santa Maria Novella, she was surprised to experience an excited buzz in the air. People were smiling and happy, joyous even. And the sun was shining again.

But surely, thirty-five people had just died in a tragedy – what was there to be happy about?

She passed another newspaper kiosk. The banner headline read:

CHI E` IL PRETE MIRACOLOSO??

'What does it say?' she asked the stall-holder.

'The priest,' said the man, grinning, 'he save them.'

'Saved who?' she demanded.

'*Tutti!*' he said with a laugh. 'All of them!'

But there was a bustle of people round the stall and the man could say no more so Natalie hurried on her way to the church – where she found a huge throng of joyful worshippers. The place was packed.

She squeezed in at the back where she learnt from the lady next to her that all the people feared crushed or drowned in the accident had simply woken up and walked away. There was talk of a mysterious priest laying his hands on the people supposed dead.

'*Il prete miracoloso,*' whispered the lady. 'The miraculous priest.'

After Mass, Natalie searched in vain for Father Francesco.

She waited until the church was empty then walked round the cloisters. No sign. Frustrated, she tried to phone him. All she got was a long *beep*.

She found herself in front of the memorial to those who died in 1966. There was a very old priest laying some flowers under the list of names. He straightened up slowly with his hand to his back. He made the sign of the cross.

'Excuse me, Father,' said Natalie softly. 'I'm sorry to intrude on your devotions but I wonder if you can help me? I'm looking for a colleague of yours, a Dominican. Father Francesco di Giorgio – do you know him?'

The old priest stood very still and gave her a funny look.

'Signora, I hope you are not here to make fun of an old man. Of course I know Francesco. We were at the seminary together.'

'Do you know where he is now?'

'Signora, this is not funny. Why do you say these things?'

'But... but I was talking to him yesterday – I said I'd meet him after Mass.'

The old priest saw Natalie's distress and realised that she was not making fun of him. 'Signora,' he said gently, 'come closer. Look.' And he pointed to the memorial to the flood victims of 1966.

There were thirty-five names.

The last name was *Francesco di Giorgio, 1901–1966.*

The old priest smiled at Natalie. 'Thirty-five lost then, thirty-five saved now. *Grazie, Francesco,*' and he slowly walked away.

Natalie's phone beeped, a text. There was no sender, only a message:

I will always be with you.

16

END COTTAGE, ORFORD

SUZIE WILDE

The taxi driver keeps firing questions at her. Ava smiles, ashamed of a spurt of anger. Maybe he's practising English for citizenship, or just lonely. The countryside looks desolate, through the rain-bobbled windows. She already misses the safety of a bustling Friday afternoon in Islington.

'Tourists gone,' he says. 'You like quiet, no?'

She nods, but this emptiness is unsettling.

'Orford best in summer.' The driver tackles a roundabout. 'Smoked salmon, ice cream, oysters.'

It's what Ava had pictured when Mark told her about this weekend away, their first. When she was small, holidays meant sandy beaches: endless, happy days.

'You like music?' He taps an ear.

'It's a podcast.' Ava gives in, and puts her AirPods away. 'Climate… stuff.'

'My boys learn guitar. You have family?'

'I live with my grandmother.'

'Is good.'

It's failure. Ava resents the easy lives of Mark's children. She wants him to be fully present, concentrating on her, instead of checking his phone in case one of them needs something. It makes her feel invisible; yet she's supposed to be always available.

Mark had called on Wednesday: 'Just booked an Airbnb at the seaside, sweetie! You'll love it: no Wi-Fi, no telly. Meet you there Friday at five.'

Her instructions arrive end-to-end encrypted, as if he's a spy: *Liverpool Street to Woodbridge. Taxi to Orford Ness. End Cottage key code 1379.*

What does she really feel about Mark? Nana says she's 'always picking wrong 'uns.' The last one made Ava doubt herself so much she's not sure what she actually feels about anything. And then the depression.

Her phone buzzes like a hornet, the screen lighting up with Mark's name.

'Hello?' She clutches the phone to her ear. 'Are you there already? I'm in the taxi, won't be too long.'

'Five, ten minutes,' the driver says.

She hates the fact he is listening but passes on the information.

'So, listen, sweetie. I'm stuck in Amersham.'

The relief is surprising. 'Don't worry, I can go home!'

'Only tonight,' Mark is talking over her, 'so I'll be at the cottage by lunchtime, latest.'

'I can't stay there on my own...'

'Hang on, sweetie.'

A woman's voice, distant. He laughs. Isn't Amersham where his daughter lives? Ava senses the driver's attention and looks out of the window, seeing only grey.

'Sorry, sweetie, gotta go.'

'No, Mark. Wait! What am I supposed to do all night with no Wi-Fi?'

'Read a book. Loads there.'

How does he know? Ava savages her thumbnail. What if his daughter – precious Lulu – owns the cottage?

The taxi driver is silent until he swings into a gravel parking space and tells her the fare. She adds a good tip, to be liked.

'Your man send bouquet, see?' He lifts his chin toward the cottage door.

Not eco-friendly. These are yellow chrysanthemums, with their smell of damp clay. Funeral flowers, Nan calls them, and won't have them in the house.

'Here.' The driver waggles a business card. 'Phone friendly taxi.'

The code releases a key. Ava steps into a bright, open room, with white walls, blond floorboards and woven, blue-striped rugs. The only sound is the polite hum of a fridge-freezer, somewhere at the back. The calm space gives her a sense of possibility, like walking into an art gallery. She could be a different person, here.

Still in her coat, she drops her bag and heads for the tall window at the quayside end of the cottage, longing to see the sea. But there is only mud, with a looming bank of shingle beyond.

The seaside is indoors. Striped pebbles are in stacks on the windowsill and larger stones on the hearth. There's a coffee table book of *THE SEA* and blue bookcases fill the fireplace alcoves. Most shelves are full of broken-spine paperbacks: thrillers, war stuff, but the wide bottom shelf holds art, cookery and local history.

One book is about Orford. Ava starts flicking through pages of photographs and a leaflet falls out: *THE NESS… Wild, remote and exposed, Orford Ness contains the ruined remnants of a disturbing past.*

It's the shingle bank outside the window. The leaflet marks a place in the book. Several images show stark concrete structures, captioned: *On the deserted Ness, secret Cold War military tests were carried out.*

She wants to see the impact on nature.

On her way out, she collects the key from a table by the hall window. There's a green booklet under some takeaway flyers, with a sea-milled stone on top. It has a perfect smooth round hole in the centre. She wonders if it is natural and reaches out. Snap! The shock of a spider-web makes her heart pound, as something huge and dark scuttles into a corner. The thing squats, legs tensed, thrumming with the intent to jump at her. Ava won't sleep if it's somewhere inside. Her hand closes round the stone and she smashes it down on the creature, hard, to be certain it's dead. Outside, she throws the stone beside the chrysanthemums and heads for the quay.

The rain has stopped but a sulphurous smell hangs in the dank air. The tide has fallen so low that the slate-grey mudflats, carved by a winding channel, stretch as far as the Ness, humped like the back of some sullen sea beast.

Ava walks briskly onto the quay, heading for a kiosk. Her sandwich on the train was hours ago. It's closed, like everything else, and she feels a growing unease. What if Mark doesn't come to Orford at all?

There's no message on her phone, which needs charging. Ava thumbs a sharp corner of the taxi card in her pocket. Would it be childish to run home to Nana? A line of masts spike the deepening sky beyond a small clubhouse. If someone is there to talk to she will stay.

The smell gets worse as she nears the sailing club: a mix of sewer and seaweed. The boats in the dinghy park are a patchwork of faded tarpaulins, apart from one, where a white-haired woman is scraping away at its hull. She is wearing an unravelling fisherman's sweater over loose, paint-spattered jeans, stuffed into black gumboots that look a few sizes too big. Perhaps the clothes belong to a dead husband.

A small terrier pokes around in the pea-shingle, then starts furious digging; stones scatter against the boat-sides.

'Archie, come back here. Archie!'

The dog breezily cocks its leg against a neighbouring dinghy and wanders off.

The woman sees Ava. 'Looking for someone?' Her face is like Nana's old leather handbag.

'No. I'm... here for the weekend...'

'End Cottage.' The woman's dog rushes through the boats, barking. 'Archie!'

Even this abruptness dooms Ava to stay. 'Is there a food store somewhere?'

'A supermarket? Most folk like the remoteness of the Ness.' It's a rebuke.

'Can I walk to a pub, or…'

'Not open. There's a fish pie in the freezer.'

Ava checks her phone. It's only five and the evening yawns ahead of her.

'Are people allowed on the Ness?'

'Best see it from the causeway, if you want a walk. There and back, or take a footpath over farmland and do a circuit.' She looks down at Ava's trainers. 'Those'll be ruined, mind, in the gaulty mud.'

'These are old,' she lies.

The woman glances toward the darkening channel. 'Don't go as far as the mill, the tide comes in fast at springs.'

'Springs?'

'City girl, are you? When the moon's pull is strongest, the tide goes out very low and comes back in very high at springs.'

'I know about the sea.' Her belittling has annoyed Ava. 'But not your name for high tides. Or mud.'

The woman assesses her. 'So tonight is a king tide, when the sea can reach End Cottage by midnight. Have you heard about the Wild Man of Orford?'

'Not yet.'

'Some fishermen caught him in their nets. He was covered in shaggy hair, and could only growl. So they kept him prisoner, up at the castle.' The woman sounds angry. 'It was torture, not letting him return to the sea.'

'When was this?'

'There's a booklet in the cottage.' The woman turns back to work. 'Best get on. Sunset in an hour.'

There is no sign of the dog. In a mad moment, Ava believes

the Wild Man has taken him. But then he rushes past her at the gate and throws himself down beside his owner.

Eight rough steps lead up to the causeway, where a stench of seaweed and wormy wood hits Ava. The extra-low tide has pulled away a veil and exposed hidden things along the shore. A distant seabird gives a rising, haunting call that reeks of loneliness. She keeps pace with a brown bird that stalks across the mudflat, occasionally probing with its long, curved beak. Other seabirds have left arrowhead patterns between rusted buckets, mangled bicycles and crumbling concrete squares. Forlorn.

It feels too like depression, so Ava crosses a stile to turn inland. After the misty rain, the low sun is making the hedgerows properly autumnal, draped in bronzed, gauzy webs. She dares to eat some late blackberries and hopes Nana is wrong about the devil.

A blackbird fixes her with its dark beadiness.

Ava taps the mandala tattoo on her wrist. 'I set my own boundaries.'

She could tell Mark that she had to rush home to look after Nana; there must be a late train. She walks on, skirting the worst mud, trying to call the taxi. There is no signal, and when the landscape opens out it's clear the path has taken her away from Orford. She heads back to the stile, cursing; snagged by bramble-whips; skidding and sliding into puddles.

The tide is filling the channel. It follows her along the shoreline, pinching and poking at the ribby carcasses of old fishing boats and fingering the dull pebbles. As she rounds a bend of the inlet, End Cottage is below. Its thin strip of grass and few pebbles surely can't protect it from the sea.

When she reaches it, Ava checks to see how close the crusted brown tide-line comes; it makes a border halfway up the grass. There is only a faint line, up against the cottage wall; the boat woman was trying to scare the silly Londoner.

'Once in a blue moon, Mrs Know-all!'

It's pure Nana.

Ava leaves her filthy trainers at the door. The holed stone and flowers are still there – but also a handwritten card: *Sweetness. I'll spoil you tomorrow!*

He always gets round her and she can never say No.

It's early evening and all the downstairs lights are on, making mirrors of the windows. Ava closes the curtains. She has already unpacked in the back bedroom; found her AirPods and phone charger; made a mug of chamomile tea and reached the end of the climate podcast without taking in a word. Being alone has made her rehearse all her bad decisions and failures.

'What you need is belly timber,' Nana would say.

Ava finds the fish pie in the freezer and a bottle of wine in the fridge. She pours a large glass and downs half of it whilst reading the instructions for an air fryer. At two hundred degrees Celsius her pie will cook in only twenty minutes.

'Cheers, Ninja!'

But her fish pie is bland, cold in the middle, with too many small bones. She pushes it aside and takes the bottle into the living space.

The woman said there was a booklet about the Wild Man, which might be the green one under the holed stone. Sure enough, its cover has a blockish woodcut of a man with writhing hair. Is he smiling or snarling? The thick, creamy pages snag on the roughness of her fingers with a scratchy sound.

Ava reads: *He longs for the sea, watching, keening, from the bars on his prison window.*

A small charge runs through her, like a trickle of electricity. She takes the stairs two at a time, up to the double bedroom that faces the Ness; she switches off the lamp and then forces up a stiff sash window.

Water holds the last memory of light. A gull arcs, its sharp cries piercing the early-evening sky. Currents pluck and pucker the water, swirling and chopping round the quay; making boats bob and curtsey at their buoys. There is a distant slatting of rigging in the soft night breeze. She was hoping for human sounds, but none come.

The window won't shut fully again. Ava stares at her tattoo.

'I invite love.' Mark can fix the sash tomorrow, and everything will be all right.

Downstairs, the booklet is open at another woodcut: *He will only eat raw food. With monstrous hands he squeezes the juices from fish and drinks them.*

The image repulses her. The lingering smell of fish pie makes Ava nauseous and she shivers, gut to scalp, like when she had flu. She hides the booklet under *THE SEA*, wishing she had never seen it. Staring at flames would be a cure; there are logs in a basket but she has no idea how to lay a fire. She decides to take the bottle of wine up to bed.

Dusk has crept deeper into the room and moonlight makes the curtain folds glow like sinew on bone. A full moon. Close to the house, a dinghy nudges against the mud with a soft sigh. Is the tide highest tonight? A creature could come out of the waves and reach the house in three bounds. Ava keeps vigil at the window, drinking, until something in her shifts.

The huge white bed is another moon. She undresses quickly, pulls back its covers and gets in. The smooth flatness of starched sheets is pleasant. She softly moves her arms and legs, swimming in a cool sea of crisp cotton. It smells of wind-dried laundry and ironing.

Ava wakes to the smell of the ocean. The window is fully open; a sudden breeze whispers of its fathomless promise. The air is crisp with ozone and the cotton sheet feels damp and heavy.

She pushes it off and the tangy air on her body is like a stolen kiss.

A dark shape rises from its crouch beside the window. Its deep, low panting makes her heart beat hard beneath her hands, which cover her breasts. Something wild is in the room.

She knew it would be; she invited it in.

Her breath quickens as the shadows shift into the blurred outline of a man, silhouetted by the full moon as he crosses the window and stops, scenting the air. He comes closer and the downy hair that covers him shines like quicksilver. He reeks of storm-force winds and waves, as thrilling as the burst of bubbles when you dive.

Ava stays completely still, in this moment of crisis. There is fear all right, but even that proves she is at last alive; every tiny hair is raised, her whole skin vital and receptive. It's close to joy.

He bends over her and softly sniffs her body. His long, salt-calloused fingers take her hand; he studies the tattoo then puts it to his mouth, which is rough as driftwood. He traces its pattern with a rasping tongue. Her pulse is a drumbeat of longing for him to test every pore of her body like this. He leans across her breasts, to nuzzle the warm crease of her armpit. She feels his hair soft, then coarse; prickle, then smooth, as he moves on to lick a long, wet line up her arm to her throat, cheeks, eyelids, hairline. He is inexorable.

Ava wants to open herself completely, to hold him closer, and forever. This yearning is a mystery to her but she wants to fall down, down, deep; arms wide like a starfish. The room is full of the growls and rattles of underwater diving. She is fathoms down, hearing drowned bells.

He pulls at her lips with sharp teeth, leaving the salt-sweet taste of blood. Faster now, he ranges her whole body, seeking out each tender part; probing with his hard tongue into her ears;

sucking the lobes and then biting them. It's too much; not what she invited in.

No, no, stop. There's hot wetness on her neck. Is it blood? *Stop this, now, please, stop.*

The Wild Man's eyes are black and empty as a shark's. His briny fingers prise apart her clenched teeth and when he presses his harsh lips against her own, her throat opens to receive the sea: salt-spume and waves; coral, sand, seaweed and shingle; moray eels, seals and orcas; seahorses, oysters, herrings and rays and all the limitless creatures of his world.

IT'S STILL EARLY when Mark arrives. He lets out a long breath, relieved to see Ava's muddy trainers at the door. Lulu frightened him last night, all her warnings about a "king tide". He should have remembered the anniversary, but his mother sounded fine when he phoned. Yet here the Ness looms; its skeletal structures a constant reminder of what his poor father suffered.

There's a skitter of gravel and a dog charges at him.

'Hello, Archie,' he says. 'Hello, Mum.'

'See this?' His mother strides past him to brandish the stone. 'Hagstone. The girl put it outside. A life for a life.'

'Mum? You know a stone can't protect you, right?' There's a satisfaction about his mother that troubles him.

'Clever of you to stay with Lulu.'

He shrugs. 'Dads are always fixing things.'

'So are mothers. As soon as I wrote that card I knew what you wanted. Rid of her.'

She has drifted so far from the shore of what's normal. His daughter was right.

The smell of the sea gets stronger as Mark climbs the stairs. He crosses the landing and pushes open the bedroom door. A body lies on the bed. It has no substance, but is as thin, grey and wrinkled as air-dried fish.

17

IN THE HEART OF THE SPINDRIFT

SARAH BURCHETT-COOK

My heart beats to the rhythm of the ocean waves. It has always been so. I feel its pulse – its ebb and flow. At times my thoughts are within the depths of the sea, yet on another day, my soul will skip joyfully along the surface in the spindrift.

It was on such a day, as the wind whipped my unruly hair into a frenzy, that I first caught sight of her. Just a glimpse. Later, I knew for certain it must have been my imagination playing tricks on me.

'MUM! You've brought half the beach in with you.'

Humph. My daughter Coral. However did I manage to raise such a neat-freak? Before I could even respond, the vacuum cleaner was whirring its way around my ankles. Her quick, multitasking mind had gathered up my hairbrush en route. She glanced disapprovingly at my long, silver locks as she handed it to me.

Coral's tone softened. 'How was your walk?'

'Refreshing.'

She studied my face as she spoke. 'Dad's coming over for dinner.'

I groaned. She never stopped hoping we'd kiss and make up. It was never going to happen. Still, Tilly and Jamie loved their granddad's visits. I couldn't deny them that. Not that I had much choice in the matter, even if it was *my* house that Coral had effectively taken charge of.

The kids rushed to greet Damian when he came through the door, crouching ready for his hugs and brandishing their Easter eggs. He glanced up at me. 'Evenin', Maggie.'

I knew my curt responding nod would set the tone for the evening, but I simply wasn't happy to see him, and that's all there was to it. Between him and my daughter, I seemed to engender some level of reproach with every comment or turn of my head. I sighed and raised my eyebrows in defiance.

I sat quietly at the head of the table as the hubbub of conversation passed rapidly back and forth across the laden dishes of rice, curry and side plates.

'You've hardly eaten a thing, Mum.'

Coral was an excellent cook, and put so much effort into every meal she put on the table.

'Sorry, dear. I'm not hungry. I have a bit of a headache,' I lied. 'I think I'll go and lie down.'

Damian stood as I stood. I'm not sure what he thought he was going to do, but I waved him back down. 'I'm fine, really.'

The whispers, as I left the dining room and headed for my bedroom, receded as I closed the door. I sighed again. There had to be more to life.

My dreams that night were intense, but as is so often the case, the details fled as soon as I opened my eyes. Beads of sweat cooled on my forehead as just one lingering image persisted – an ethereal face in the spindrift. Yesterday, on the beach, it was just a flash, and then it was gone. Now, though, I could see the face clearly in front of me. Deep-blue eyes, pink lips, high cheekbones, green hair – no, blue – no, pink – it changed in the light as the sea rose and fell beyond. So strange then, not a still picture but a moving, living image.

It was early. No one else was up yet, and the weak sun of early spring was just rising above the horizon. I dressed, crept to the patio door and headed back onto the beach behind the house.

Once again the wind whipped the tops of the waves. I sat on the cold sand and pulled my shawl tight around me as I watched. But nothing. Just the cold blue sea and the foam left at my feet like an offering as the waves ebbed.

'Mum! Whatever are you doing out here? It's freezing. You're shivering. Come on, let's go indoors and I'll run you a hot bath.'

I didn't say anything. I just let Coral lead me back into the house.

I'm not sure what I'd expected that morning, but still, the ocean, as ever, filled me with peace. Coral's worried expression indicated she wasn't so calm.

'I think you should talk to someone, Mum.'

'Talk to who, dear?'

'I don't know, a counsellor maybe.'

'Why?'

'Ever since you and Dad broke up, or actually before then I suppose, you've just seemed so – distant. I think you might be suffering from depression.'

Her absurd assertion jolted me. I stared at her concerned face. 'Is that what you think? Really?'

'Dad said you were getting quieter and less interested in life with every passing day. He was really upset when you asked him to leave, you know.'

That they'd been discussing me behind my back niggled, but I was determined to take the high ground.

'Your dad had a version of me in his head that I was never able to fulfil – push and pull as he might. In the end, I'd had enough of it. I was never going to entertain his business partners and their trophy wives. I was never going to plaster my face in make-up or wear trendy clothes. He thought me beautiful when I was young, but that was all he ever liked about me.'

The blood drained from Coral's face. 'That's not true and you know it. He loves you. And, by the way, you are still beautiful.'

That little morale boost made me smile, but there seemed little point in pursuing this conversation, so I decided to bring it to an end. 'I am not depressed, I am just quiet – it's my nature to be so. I am perfectly happy, and I will not be seeing a shrink.'

'But...'

'No "buts", that's an end to it.'

It was almost three months later when I had the dream image again, and once more I headed down to the beach. It was warmer now. The summer sun heated the sand from early in the morning. There was no wind today, and the sea was flat calm, blue, and starting to warm up nicely. I raised my full skirt and tied a makeshift knot in the material to keep it out of the water as I paddled in the shallows.

Tilly and Jamie came and joined me, equipped with buckets, spades, bellyboards, towels and a tube of factor fifty, that I dutifully applied to their backs after they'd nearly depleted it on the fronts of their little bodies. I watched them as they played happily all morning. Then we went home to get some lunch. But the face in the spindrift remained in the forefront of my mind, so later, when the kids had gone to bed, and Coral sat watching the TV, I found myself once more heading out the door, pulling my shawl across my shoulders as I went.

It was a little windier now, so my hope was that I would see *her* again. Was it just my vivid imagination? Was I looking for something that simply could not be? It didn't matter. I had to try to see her again.

It was a warm evening. I didn't need the shawl after all, so I laid it on the ground and sat on it so it didn't blow away. I'm not sure how long I stayed there; it must have been a while as the sky was turning a brilliant orange. In June, that meant it was late. As usual, my mind drifted in time to the ebb and flow of the waves, and I found myself in a semi-meditative state. When I was young, I meditated a lot. Why did I stop? Damian, I suppose – that definitely wouldn't have fitted into his world.

'Maggie.'

What? Who?

'Maggie.'

The voice was close by, yet I couldn't see anyone.

'Come with me, Maggie.'

'Who's there?'

A wave rose in front of me. It manifested into a woman. Into *her*. Her sea-coloured hair flowed in the breeze. It was dry somehow. Her blue eyes were like deep, shining pools. Her peaches-and-cream complexion glowed in the light of the sunset, and her lips – her lips touched mine.

Before I knew what was happening, I was on my feet. She led me by the hand to the water, then turned and smiled back at me. I knew joy, the like of which I could not have imagined. I would follow her anywhere.

Somewhere in the back of my mind I knew this wasn't right, that I couldn't live in the sea with this woman. But I didn't care. The waves caressed me. She caressed me. I wasn't cold. I didn't choke on the water. There were others there, under the waves. I was content.

MAGGIE'S BODY was never recovered. All that remained was her shawl, discarded on the beach. Coral went back to the spot where it had been found. As she looked out to sea, she could have sworn she saw her mum's face in the spindrift. But that was just wishful thinking. She sighed as a single tear tracked down her cheek and then she went home. Her dad was coming over for dinner and she needed to get started with the baking.

18

MOTHER

MICHAEL THAME

December 2nd, 1800

My Darling Wife,

It is but a day since I left you and our cherished children, yet it feels like eternity already. I cannot come to terms with the fact we shall be apart for an entire month, worse still that I shall miss Christmas with Young Tomas, Geraint and Gwen. I look at their portraits hourly. We really are so lucky to have the pictures Old Sam drew for us. He is a first-rate artist and I do believe I will be able to see how the children have aged once I return to Kingheriot.

After the kind of calm crossing we had no right to expect in the month of December, we conducted our detail with Roberts and Williams in the most orderly of fashions and Griffith and I undertook to familiarise ourselves with our home for the next four weeks, God willing the weather. Our dwellings on Smalls Island are surprisingly comfortable and the lighthouse really is something of a wonder. I have not worked on one such as this before, and it looks as though it should not stand at all. The design, as you know, is one of stilts and a central ladder rising to a trap door in the lighthouse keepers' living quarters. The weather has thus far set so fair that I have not witnessed the spectacle of the sea rushing over the island, submerging it from view as we look down upon it. I fancy I will feel a little numb when I do. There is something of the notion of not seeing land at all that I find disagreeable.

Perhaps it is why I never sought to join the navy?

Griffith has shown himself to be capable of kindness and decency. I was very much worried that we would find ourselves adversaries in this tiny space and, of course, we are but one day in, but I think the circumstances have caused him to consider himself. After we looked over the lighthouse keepers' room and set the lamp for the night (I say night, but it became dark sometime after three of the clock) we partook of a keepers' meal and sat down to our thoughts. We were temperate in our drinking, and convivial in our conversation. We spoke of the war in India and other such events, but it is a peculiarity of lighthouse keeping, that time can stand so still when you are cut off from civilisation for however long. What we discussed last night might already be incorrect so far as the truth is concerned.

The nights here are long. Seemingly longer even than when on land. We have nothing to hear but the rushing of the wind, not that there has been much, or the wash of the sea against these tiny, but deadly, rocks. Sometimes the quarters creak to remind oneself of the precarious nature of this dwelling. It is such monotony that is somehow different at all hours that is difficult to embrace. That, and the desire to be in your arms once more.

I write in the hope that you will be able to read this before you see me once more. The thought of you having no contact from me for a month or more fills me with dread and disquiet, for it will mean I do not receive your letters if you have not received mine if the sea has been too heavy.

But I shall not think about that. I shall think about you and our darling children. I shall think about our home and your daily rituals as I do mine. I shall think about the time when I return to land and to Wales and to you. I have never understood whether it allows time to pass more quickly or not. But it is something I have always done.

Love always, your faithful Tomas.

December 25th, 1800

My Darling Wife,

Today, of all days, the loneliest in the world. The violence of weather has remained since that first becalmed week and Griffith and I have not spoken to another soul in almost four.

I can happily relate that Griffith remains convivial except when he partakes a little much of the grog. I limit myself to one bottle of beer at daybreak and another at fall of night. My share of the supply shall last me until February, but I fear that will not be the same for Griffith. I can only hope that we are visited long before then. Despite our comfortable parlay, I have seen on occasion the Devil enter him and his anger rise a little. I find it strange that such a man as he should change so much from the person we both know and dread when on land.

I watch him closely to see any sign he will alter in his ways. I would like him to lower his drink, not only to consider our supplies but also to avoid the unpleasantness that will surely come from his drinking too much. It is not as though we have not seen this with our own eyes before. But some men need the comfort of drink to pass through a challenge such as this and Griffith is of that countenance. He is an experienced man, however, and I do not think he would be employed as senior lighthouse keeper if he was unable to pass the test of time. Perhaps I remain too cautious?

My heart aches for your touch and for the chance to hold our darling children. I long to have a sword fight with Young Tomas, or to chase after Geraint. I imagine he is falling less and running more, even though it has been but four weeks. And Gwen. I do not know why, but a tear always pricks at my eye when I think of her in a way that does not occur when I think of the boys. I wonder if it is that she is so young and she will have changed the most when I return? Or is it that a father feels differently for his daughter? I imagine the boys' faces as you give them the presents I fashioned for them. I can just see Young Tomas's wide eyes as you hand him the sword I made or Geraint's look of wonder when you show him how the top spins. Poor Gwen will not understand a father's love, but I *hope she takes to the wooden pegs she can hold on to or perhaps chew?*

And what of our cups? I think of the time we will be able to sit by our fireside and drink to our health with those cups. There are none other like them in the entire world. Just you and I with our cups and our grog and our children sleeping and the weather set fair or ill outside. Oh, how I think of the lane and the high hedgerows. For some reason I think of them in spring, or summer. Never now in the darkness of winter. It is an odd thought. Darkness is when I shall most like to sit by the fireside and drink and yet the hedgerows are in bloom. I do not know why I think like this.

I am so lonely here with just Griffith. But the weather has made things much worse. I pray twice daily for an end to this storm, for some chance to speak to another human being, or to receive your letters and send you mine. The wind is howling as I write. It never seems to stop. The sound of the sea is no longer gentle for it roars over the rocks. Howls and roars. And whistling. I have tried to repair any holes I have found in the dwelling, to stop the shrieks of the wind should they spring up, but there are too many. I repair one with a little cloth or parchment, and another hole screams forth when the wind changes slightly. Sometimes I think the wind is taunting us. Sometimes I fancy I hear a voice on the wind as if it has carried from land and settled on my ears. I know it is nonsense, of course. At times I can barely hear Griffith as he shouts above the din. He is but three yards from me. But I do fancy I hear voices. Perhaps they are the Sirens?

They frighten me. I hope I am not going a little mad.

Your ever loving Tomas.

December 28th, 1800

My Darling Wife,

The storm will not abate and I am afraid. Griffith does not look well. His skin seems to have become parchment and he sweats continuously. He insists it is nothing but I can see it and he worsens daily. I have taken to raising the distress signal, but he tries to take the flag down as quickly. He says there is no need as no one is able to come. He is right about that and I am fearful. And still he insists he is well.

I take solace in the lighting of the lamps for it is what I am employed to do. But Griffith does not assist me often. He is too weak and his breathing rasps. It is all he can do to reach for the grog of which he still drinks too much. The one light in this darkness is that drinking seems difficult for him and he cannot consume much, at least, it takes him a long time to finish a bottle. He still goes beyond his ration, but he does not drink so much that he becomes drunk. Yet he is angry. If he had the strength I have no fear he would try to fight and I have no desire for that.

He looks at me as though I am looking for an opportunity to harm him. It is nonsense, but there is no trust in his eyes, only devilment. I bring my pipe to my mouth and the movement makes him cower. He pulls his ale to his chest as if I am looking to take it for myself. Sometimes he starts to talk to himself. He looks into the lights and I see the reflection in his eyes as his lips move, but I can hear no more than a whisper and the words do not reach me.

When he sleeps he watches me with one eye until at last his strength fails and that one eye also closes. Then only his breathing. Short, choking sounds as his chest rises and falls. His breath rattles then there will be silence, enough for me to start to rise to check if he is still among the living, before a great snort or sudden gasp as if his body has only then remembered to take air. He thrashes in his bed. The dreams seem vivid and occasionally he cries out. He says one word, or rather name, that I can discern: Charlotte. I do not know of any Charlotte he may know. Perhaps it is a former lover, or a child lost? I wonder whether it would be fair to ask Martha if it was the former or the latter. But then she is a tough woman to be married to this man. Should I ever get off this godforsaken rock, I doubt I will seek out her counsel. Perhaps Griffith will improve and I can ask him in a moment of lucidity?

I watch him as I write. I realise I watch him continuously. I cannot say when I last slept well. But

I have to watch him, always, for I fear what he may do.

Yours ever, Tomas.

January 4th, 1801

My Darling Wife,

Griffith is DEAD! In everything that is holy, Alwyn Griffith is dead and I am the sole witness to his parting. A great dread falls over me. The storm never abates and the mania in my head gets worse. What more can the good Lord throw at a man?

Griffith went outside, in one of his incoherents, and raged at the storm that torments us so. He had done this increasingly and I was not thinking of him when I became aware of the length of his absence. It seemed too long, so I put on my overclothing and opened the door to the rail that encircled the lamp. The storm tore at my greatcoat and trousers and the wind took my breath away. It was all I could do to hold on to the rail and work my way round as rain spattered against the glass of the lamp as though thrown a bucket at a time. Spray shone ghostly in the light sent out into the far reaches of the darkness that surrounds the lighthouse and afore long I came across the fallen form of Griffith. I went to him to assist him to his feet, but he did not move. I pushed him, shouted at him and held on to the rail as it slowly dawned on me there was no life in his body. I knew in that moment I had to get him back to our quarters in case there was a chance to save him. He lay face down, with the soles of his boots toward me. I crouched and, with one hand on the rail I used the other to tug at a boot top. He came to me easily and I wondered for the wetness of the platform's assistance. I rose, but afore I took a step backwards to repeat the manoeuvre, I noticed the dark pool on the walkway just as it started to wash away in the rain and wind. I crouched again and pulled again and in short order I managed to get Griffith back into our quarters. I raised him up and put him on his bed. His eyes were open and stared ceilingwards, but there was no life in them. With the large gash across his left temple, and the heavy river of blood flowing there, I wondered if he had slipped and caught his head on the rail. I tried to sit him up, to pour a little grog in his mouth, to bandage the wound and stop the flow, but he remained lifeless. I listened for his breath and none came. He collapsed backwards when I released him and I noted suddenly that he already seemed cold. He was stone dead.

I sit here writing this letter and staring at Griffith's prone form lying on his bed. In the half-light he appears but a bundle of rags, save for the boots that point upwards, making it obvious I am looking at a corpse.

My own comportment has surprised me. There is a bottle of ale at my elbow and it is not mine. The ale ration was split between us whence we arrived and we each placed our own in the base of our own storage cupboards. My stores are considerably fuller than Griffith's, but I felt an urge to help myself. I know not why, but I have come to terms with his death with more haste than I would expect. Once I had calmed from the initial shock, I removed my greatcoat and trousers and set them to dry, then I sat back in my chair and lit a pipe. Sitting there I felt a lightness envelop me. The wind seemed softer, the rain less harsh. The air in the quarters was somehow clean, despite the corpse of Griffith. The weight gone from my shoulders was more than the weight of my greatcoat removed. I no longer had fear and I was already lonely. I realised then that I was happier he was dead.

This night I feel as well as I have done in days. This night I think of you, my Darling, and of Young Tomas, Geraint and Gwen. I know that on the morrow things will have to be done, but for now I can rest knowing that no harm will come at me from the hands of Alwyn Griffith.

Yours ever, Tomas.

January 23rd, 1801

My Darling Wife,

I have resisted the urge to burden you, but I know not what to do. Since Griffith fell, I have lived in a strange world of indifference and repulsion. I desired to keep his body in the quarters for I realised I could not bury him at sea as must be the custom. What will happen when my relief comes? Our quarrels with the Griffiths are well-known, and I am still sore over the fine I received for the fighting he fomented in the Royal George. There are long memories and tongues will talk.

Soon after his death I felt it was not the fall that had killed him, for the wound on his temple was but an inch across when I cleansed it. It is now my belief his heart gave out and the wound was incidental, caused, as I contend, by striking the handrail as he fell. As such, I determined to keep Griffith in my quarters until salvation comes and the body can be considered by a coroner, thus absolving me of any fault in his death.

For two days I was resigned to the sight of Griffith lying motionless under the bedsheet with which I had covered him. I confess I did not find it difficult, for one of my two great enemies at Smalls was no more. The storm persisted, but I no longer felt threatened from within as well as without. But his corpse started to smell after three days and I realised I had to do more than leave him where I had placed him the night of his death. I chose to bound him more tightly. I am unaware of how long a body can remain before it does not give up any assistance to a coroner, but I determined that to wrap him in rags would both add to the preservation and limit the stench that had started to come from him. I began by removing the *outer clothes in which he had died and the experience was not one on which I wish to dwell. Suffice to say that I left his undergarments in place and wrapped his bedsheets as tightly around him as I could. It was difficult, and I had to break his left arm at the elbow for it stuck out and made the wrapping more onerous. I was much happier when he had been but a bundle of old clothes under the bedsheet, for now I could see the outline of a man.*

But the stench remained. I burnt his clothes and boots to remove the thick scent of death coming from them. I was happy to do so as I feared for my wood and coal ration. Whenever the storm chose to blow in a different direction, I would open the door to the elements and wish away the black air in the quarters. But that air returned as soon as the wind changed and I had to close the door against the fury. At night I blocked my nostrils with cloth, but could taste his putrid corpse instead. I drank ale to remove that sensation and was frequently sick. I took to going outside for as long as I could stand, just to get the sweet freshness into my lungs. But the stench never left me and neither did the storm. Even on the clearer days, when the sun almost appeared, the wind did not cease and the swell covered the rocks beneath me. There was no respite.

I kept the lamp burning and the distress signal remained at hoist. I saw ships come within three or four lengths of cable and I waved ahoy. I saw move-

ment on their decks and I hoped they would realise my torment and precipitate my rescue. But then I looked at the rocks a hundred feet below and knew that no boat could land.

The stench has got worse. Despite all attempts to rid the quarters of death, the smell remains and has become unbearable. Today, I moved Griffith's corpse and tied it tight to the rail outside. It is but a temporary measure. I will construct a coffin using the wood from his bed and wardrobe and place him in it. I shall fix that coffin to the rail outside and continue my duties with a wall between Griffith and I.

This storm cannot continue forever. It has lasted four weeks or more already. Squalls are fewer and rain less common. I lament the rain as I eye the remaining ale with some trepidation. The supply has fallen more quickly than I realised. Perhaps Griffith had drunk more than I thought? Or perhaps I am drinking more? My head is fuddled this day, and I cannot remember how many ales I consumed last night. I remember throwing empty bottles into the black sea below me, but I confess I do not recall going abed. Thus I need that rainwater or I fear I may die of thirst if the storm continues much longer. I laugh at that. And I laugh now. Dying of thirst in the middle of the ocean! I wonder again why the good Lord has seen fit to punish me this way.

The lamp is lit till morning, and I have ale to settle

me. I will commence the building of the coffin on the morrow.

Yours, Tomas.

February 16th, 1801

My Darling,

Still he mocks me! I have built a coffin for him, affixed him to the outer rail and prayed for him and yet he will not leave me in peace!

The building of the coffin was a simple task and I had it completed in a little over a day. I placed Griffith's body (which had gone completely stiff after the two nights it spent lashed to the rail) within and sealed the lid. I had not quite the right tools, but the wood was solid and I found the nails I needed. I settled the coffin against the rail and hammered it in place. I chose to place it furthest from the doorway so that I had least worry about coming across it. I wish I had thought more. Griffith now lies immediately above my bed at night. And he bangs heavily in the wind.

Had I the forethought, I would have used the wood from my own bed for his coffin and slept in his, although as I write these words, the abhorrence of sleeping in a dead man's bed overcomes me. I have still not rid myself of the stench of decay although I wonder if it is there at all and I am imagining it. Will it ever leave me? I still get that putrid taste when I eat, or drink.

And I have drunk much. I found hidden in the edges of Griffith's bed three bottles of whisky. I was overcome when I found them. I had prayed many times, so many times for salvation both for his soul and mine and then I found the whisky. I have drunk more than I ever have before. The first bottle went that first night. I resolved with querulous head not to allow myself a full bottle again. I don't remember when I drank the second bottle. The last night of January I realised I had the last bottle of whisky and eight bottles of ale left. I had already gone through the remainder of Griffith's ration. The coffin banged against the outer rail in yet more bl—dy wind and I cried again. My nightmare never ending. I resolved then to drink the lot, to Hell with it all. Should I fall from that outer rail, so be it, I thought. I drank. I screamed into the night and I drank some more. I remember laughing into that strange darkness beyond the reach of the lamp and watched in vain as I tried to follow each empty bottle's flight as I thrust it out to sea. I saw none land. I awoke on the floor, the door swinging wildly in the wind, slamming against its frame but not catching. The latch had broken in the night. And then I became aware of more banging as the wind rushed into the quarters and fouled the inside, cupboards opening and closing, clothes strewn about, whether by my hand or not I could not tell. I repaired the latch and began the slow process of clearing the room, collecting papers, maps, even metal *spoons that had been flung about. Could the wind shift a metal spoon, or was I looking at destruction I myself had wrought?*

The room decorous, I checked on the lamp and the distress signal. Much more wind and there will be little left of that flag. The day was lighter, but the gusts kept up and the swell washed over the Smalls. I fancied I could see a ship some distance to the south but I had seen so many, nothing and no one had come and nothing and no one would be able to land in the swell. I turned away and went back into the quarters... to the sound of more banging. At first I could not tell where it came from and then I happened to look out of the window above my bed, to where I had placed Griffith's coffin against the outer rail. I saw that it moved. The constant shrieking wind had begun to work the coffin loose. I knew I could not go back to it.

I look through the window now. The coffin rocks on its side. Duh-duh... duh-duh... duh-duh... It never stops as the wind never stops. I no longer hear the whistling through the gaps in the quarters, or the crash of wave upon rock, but the coffin? Duh-duh... duh-duh... duh-duh... like the thrumming of fingers on a table, or the steady rhythm of a heartbeat.

It's Griffith. Even in death he will not leave me alone.

Tomas.

March 12th, 1801

I feel the hand of death upon me. And I see the hand of death in front of me! It beckons me!

IT BECKONS ME!

Never has a man wanted the end to arrive as quickly as I do now. The storm has worsened again and the coffin has been smashed to pieces. I awoke in darkness and realised I had allowed the lamp to extinguish. I rushed out and did my duty against the elements. It would have been the work of a moment to throw myself backwards and over the rail. But I thought of the glory of God and I thought of our children. And so I desired to live. But then I returned to the quarters and immediately I saw it. White, not quite skeleton, with wisps of flesh still clinging, an eerie grey skin flapping and a hand motioning backwards and forth.

'Come,' it said. I fancied I heard the word spoken and I cowered. 'Come!' I was sure the word was real in my head. Above the constant roar from outside I heard that one word. And as I looked on in horror I realised something else. It was the voice of Griffith. I do not know how long I stood and stared at that spectral hand as it moved backward and forth and beckoned me to come. I recall falling to my knees, unable to turn away my gaze. The fingernails had turned black and seemed to be rather long. I fixated on this as I cried and cried until no more tears would come. The world seemed to disappear from around me. All I could see was the hand. 'Come,' all I could hear. I tried to turn my head but I couldn't. Back and forth the hand moved. Back and forth. 'Come.'

At last I broke the spell. I knew what had happened and I knew that Griffith had planned it all. The coffin was strong, but it was now smashed to pieces. I had wrapped him tightly, but the wind had played the very Devil and his wrappings were but rags now. And the hand dangling, beckoning back and forth. I had broken that arm at the elbow and now it had come free and tapped at the window above my bed, beckoning.

I did not sleep that night. I am not sure I have slept since. I want death and I do not think it far from me now. I try to work out how long I have been trapped here, with the corpse of a man I did not like and with the corpse of a man who torments me still. I maintain the lamp, but I cannot take much more. There is little biscuit left and I cannot collect enough water when it does rain. I no longer look at the sea for that mocks me also. So much water I cannot drink. I think of you and of our children and no longer know how I feel. You have my undying devotion, but now you seem...

I cannot bear this any longer. I pray you read these words.

Your Loving Tomas.

March 29th, 1801

Mother,

I am gone.

The hand is still there. Night after night it mocks me. I dare not go near it and yet I must light the lamp. I have done my duty by that lamp and I have done my duty by my wife and children. I hope I have been a son you can be proud of.

But I am weak now. The pen feels heavy in my hand, the words blurred when before I could see. It is four months since I set foot on this place forgotten by God and reclaimed as Hell on Earth by the Devil. Four months of torture that no man could take.

Damn Alwyn Griffith! But I have done my duty by him.

Goodbye, Mother.

Tomas.

'How do you think he died, sir?'

The storm had finally abated. A boat had been despatched and landed on the Smalls. Edward Llewellyn looked at the figure hunched at the stern of the jolly boat that had brought them to the tiny rocky island. It had taken some time to coax the terrified man from the quarters and he was so weak he had to be lashed to one of the relief keepers who carried him on his back down the treacherous ladder that descended to the sea-streaked rocks below the lighthouse. The shrouded figure found partly mummified on the outer rail of the lighthouse's living quarters was in the process of being lowered down by rope. A bedsheet was used as a makeshift sack as the gruesome cargo was transported across the rocks.

In his more than thirty years working for Trinity House, Llewellyn had come across the bodies of many. Usually they were drowned sailors, but sometimes lighthouse keepers. None had been as horrific a scene as this. No one had set foot on the Smalls since Griffith and Howell four months prior, and unprecedented storms had stopped anyone from getting anywhere near them ever since.

'I ask, sir, because I've known Tomas Howell since we were boys. I consider him a good friend. I wonder if you know how he died.'

Llewellyn looked at Rhys John, the man asking the questions of him. He looked again at the sheets of papers carefully folded in his hand and placed them in the inside pocket of his greatcoat. The relief keepers passed, carrying the bedsheet sack between them and approached the jolly boat.

The scream pierced the tranquil spring air. Above the sounds of a gently lapping swell the relief keepers stopped as they held the bedsheet over the bow. The figure in the stern screamed again. But he didn't move. The relief keepers pulled back from the screaming and placed their burden on the sodden rocks in front of the boat.

'The truth will out, John,' Llewellyn said, patting the breast of his greatcoat where he had safely stowed the letters. 'But it is not Tomas Howell who is dead.'

19

ECHOES FROM THE FLANNAN ISLES

JOSS MOWFORTH

In December 1900, the relief ship *Hesperus* set sail for the Flannan Isles, a scattered cluster of rocks and sea cliffs in the Outer Hebrides. Her mission was routine: deliver supplies and bring home the lighthouse crew who had been stationed there for a month.

Storms delayed the journey by over a week.

When the vessel finally reached Eilean Mòr, the largest of the Flannan Isles, on the 26th of December, something was amiss. The lighthouse stood tall above the cliffs, but no flag flew from the pole. No welcome party waited on the landing stage. The only movement came from seabirds wheeling overhead.

The island was silent.

A search party climbed the steep path to the lighthouse and found the building locked. Inside, everything was in place. Clocks had stopped. The hearth was cold. A meal had been laid out on the table, untouched. A chair lay overturned. One of the oilskin coats still hung by the door.

There was no sign of Principal Keeper James Ducat, Second Assistant Thomas Marshall, or Occasional Keeper Donald McArthur.

The three men had vanished without a trace.

The official inquiry suggested they had been swept out to sea during a violent storm, possibly whilst trying to secure loose equipment on the west landing. But the explanation satisfied few. The steep cliff face showed no signs of a rockfall. There were no footprints. No wreckage washed ashore.

Only the logbook remained, its final pages strange and fragmented. It spoke of powerful winds, of unnatural silence, of a creeping dread that seemed to hang over the island like the fog itself. The final entry was dated the 15th of December.

No bodies were ever found.

No conclusive answer has ever been given.

. . .

I REMEMBER the fog most of all.

It came in thick and low, swallowing the sea and blurring the coastline from the tower. At first, we thought little of it; fog is no stranger to Flannan, and the work goes on regardless. We kept to our routine. Topped up the oil. Took our turns on watch. Cooked our meals. Wrote the log.

Yet the fog did not lift.

The others called it *haar*, a word they knew from the east coast. That damp sea-fog that creeps in silent and grey. I'd never used the word myself, not growing up with it, but it fit. The way it coiled around the lantern room. The way it surrounded you.

By the third day it clung to the skin, heavy and wet, like the breath of something sleeping just out of sight. Sound dulled. Colours drained. Even the gulls – noisy, ugly things that they were – disappeared.

Then the other birds came.

They arrived just before dusk, slipping out of the haar without a sound. I saw them first from the lantern room. There were three of them, perched on the rocks by the west landing. They weren't like any seabird I'd ever seen. It was difficult to tell from that distance. They appeared taller than a man, with wings folded like cloaks. Feathers black, but with an oily sheen that shimmered green when the lantern caught them.

They didn't move. They didn't make a sound.

We watched them for a while. Marshall said they looked like omens. Ducat said nothing at all. I remember feeling... unsettled. Not afraid. Not yet. Just something in the gut. Like a dream you don't realise is a dream until it starts to turn.

Later that evening, I went down toward the landing with the intention of getting a closer look. I hadn't taken more than ten steps when the birds rose together, gliding out over the water in perfect silence.

And then – they dropped. Straight down, into the sea, without a splash.

The next evening the birds were back. Perched in the same place. Watching.

They came every evening after that, just before sunset. Three dark shapes in the fog, unmoving. We stopped joking about them. Marshall muttered that they were sentries. Ducat, once so precise in his habits, started keeping odd hours. He would rise in the middle of the night and pace the corridor in the living quarters at the base of the lighthouse. I heard him whispering to himself once, though I couldn't make out the words.

The fog thickened. The light from the lantern barely reached the rocks. Sometimes we thought we saw flashes – not lightning, but something pale and pulsing far out at sea. Not natural. Too steady. Too quiet.

The supply boat wasn't due for days. I stopped writing in the log. What was there to say? That we were afraid of birds? That the air had gone still? That the silence at night no longer felt empty, but full?

It was the evening of the 15th when the quiet began to feel different.

There had been no birds that day. Not on the rocks. Not in the air. The haar had thickened until the sea and sky became the same grey void. Inside, we kept to routine. Habit was all we had left.

I stirred the stew while Marshall laid out the bowls. Ducat was by the window, staring into nothing. The lamp in the kitchen flickered every so often, not enough to be strange, but enough to notice.

The conversation had dried up days before. We moved around each other like ghosts. When we sat down to eat, no one touched their food. We were waiting for something. I don't think any of us could have said what.

Then Ducat stood, slowly, and walked to the door. He didn't speak. Just opened it, and stared out into the fog. Marshall followed him. After a moment, I got up too, but caught my foot on the leg of the chair as I pushed back. It clattered behind me. I didn't look to see where it landed. Outside, the fog hung low over the ground. I could barely see past the path. But I knew what they were looking at.

They were there again. The same three shapes. Still as stone. Closer this time.

None of us spoke.

We stood there for I don't know how long, the cold creeping into our sleeves. The shapes didn't move. Neither did we. I could hear the stew bubbling behind us in the kitchen, quiet and steady, as though nothing at all had changed.

Then one of the shapes tilted its head.

Not fast. Not sudden. Just a slow, deliberate shift, as though it had only now remembered we were watching.

Ducat took a step forward. Marshall called after him, but too softly. Even his voice was afraid to carry too far. Ducat didn't turn. He just kept walking, slowly and carefully, down the path toward the landing. There was no reason to follow. And yet, without thinking, I stepped out after him – just behind Marshall, our boots finding the path together. The haar swallowed us quickly. By the time we reached the slope, I could no longer see the light from the tower. I could barely see the ground beneath my boots.

The birds remained ahead of us. Always the same distance. Never moving, and yet never closer. Then the light changed.

The haar lit up all at once but not from the lantern, nor from the moon. From nowhere. From everywhere. Pale and green, but not a green I recognised. It made the rocks shine slick like glass.

Marshall gasped. Ahead, Ducat stopped moving. The birds began to rise. Not flapping, just rising. They lifted straight up into the air, impossibly smooth, like gravity had forgotten them.

The noise came next. I use the word noise but it does not describe the sensation. I felt it in my teeth. In my ribs. A pressure building behind the eyes. Marshall fell to his knees. I tried to get to him, but my legs wouldn't move.

And then everything dropped. The ground. The light. The sky. All of it, gone in an instant, like someone had yanked the island out from under us.

I awoke to stillness. No wind. No sea. No fog.

I was lying on a smooth surface, hard but not cold, beneath a sky I did not recognise. It wasn't dark, but there was no sun – just a constant silver glow, as though the air itself gave off light.

I sat up. My limbs worked, though they felt lighter than they should. Marshall was nearby, curled on his side, unmoving but breathing. Ducat stood a little way off, staring into the distance.

And there they were.

The birds (or what we had called birds) were no longer shrouded in fog. Their wings were folded back, their forms taller than I remembered, more angular. Feathers that weren't feathers shimmered with impossible colour. From the crowns of their heads, strands of golden light spiralled slowly upwards, twisting and dividing like liquid threads.

They stood silently, watching us.

One stepped forward. I expected fear, but it didn't come. A presence brushed gently against my thoughts, not speaking, but *showing*. Images, shapes, patterns beyond language. A sense of scale that stretched too far to hold.

I could feel Ducat and Marshall beside me. Whatever we were seeing, we were seeing together.

Space stretched out before us, but not the kind we had known. Not sky or sea or distance. It was more like looking into a vast memory; not mine but something older. Languages unfolded in shape and light. Worlds flickered in and out of being, each more alien than the last.

The presence didn't speak. But understanding came, fast and vast.

I became aware that we were not the first. Others had stood where we now stood. Others had been shown. Civilisations long gone. Creatures whose names we would never know. Some had understood. Some had tried to resist. Some had simply disappeared. Now it was our turn.

We were not to return to Eilean Mòr, or the Earth for that matter. Not just yet.

We had to be shown what lay beyond the narrow lanes of human thought. Energy without end. Motion without decay. The shaping of stars. The folding of time. We were given glimpses of the impossible. It was a gift.

But even then, a question stirred. What was their motive? A need to be known? To be remembered? To connect? Or simply to leave something of themselves behind – not out of kindness, but instinct?

Time passed, though not in any way I could measure. We no longer spoke, but we understood one another. There was no hunger, no pain, no sleep. Only learning. Only seeing.

Ducat embraced it first. I remember the moment he began to drift. He unravelled gently into the current of whatever passed for time in that place. His outline shimmered, and then he was simply part of the light.

Marshall held on longer. His eyes still searched, still questioned, but whatever he saw, it drew him deeper. His thoughts began to echo with theirs, smooth and strange. He stopped looking at me. He stopped needing to.

But I could not let go.

Even surrounded by wonder, even as knowledge poured through me, Earth still called. I could feel it – the wind on the cliffs, the salt on my tongue, the weight of my oilskin coat. A pull I could not shake. The thought of home, distant and faded, but insistent.

The presence felt it too. There was no resistance. Only observation. As though it had seen this before.

I don't remember the parting. Only the sense of falling. Not fast. Not violent. Just drifting away from that great, impossible place.

And then, I awoke.

Not in the lighthouse. Not on the island. I was lying on wet grass on the coast. Hills rose in the distance. There was the scent of heather in the air, and the sound of gulls. Noisy, ugly gulls. I knew I was home.

I staggered to my feet, weak but unhurt. I didn't recognise the place. A farmer found me not long after, near a low stone wall by a sheep path. He said I looked like I'd been caught in a storm. I told him nothing.

Time was harder to place. Days passed in a blur. Then years. I was taken in, given shelter, food, a place to rest. People assumed I'd been shipwrecked. I let them. However, my mind was clearer than ever.

The things I'd seen. The things I now knew. I could feel it humming beneath the surface; equations unwritten, machines I had never seen, patterns in the sky that now made perfect sense. They had given me knowledge. Or at least the outline of it. I could barely write fast enough to capture what rushed through me.

I began to make plans. With this knowledge, I could be rich. Not just comfortable, but untouchable. I sketched designs I didn't fully understand. Drew up ideas for power sources, engines, systems of motion. I sent letters, made enquiries.

I looked west. Where else could a man start again? The New World, they called it. Opportunity, wealth, expansion. America.

I booked passage on a liner. I boarded without ceremony. No farewells. Just the quiet satisfaction of a man who knew things others did not. A man stepping into the future.

Now, I lie here, on a bed that has never been slept in before. I run my hands over the fine linen and trace the curve of the carved woodwork. There's a painting above the writing desk: a ship at sea, cutting through a storm. It feels apt.

The cabin is silent save for the faint rhythm of engines far below. The band plays somewhere above, muffled and cheerful. I feel the warmth of the expensive wine numb my senses. Imagine it. My story. From lonesome, poor, humble lighthouse keeper to this: lying on my four-poster bed in the middle of the Atlantic, caviar and wine in my belly. 'The world is my oyster,' I whisper. The warmth from the wine rises to my head. I think I will go to sleep now.

Turning, I reach over to the lamp beside my bed. What an amazing vessel this is – everything is perfect, not a detail missing. A symbol of my new life, I suppose. The designer didn't miss an inch of this ship. He never even failed with the delicate artistry of the bedside lamp. The marvellous lampshade of entwined flowers was supported by a great brass stand for the orb of light. The brass has been cast completely smooth save for the engraved name of the ship through the middle. What a great name; short yet powerful. Simply the greatest name for the greatest ship ever to sail the waves. Just one word.

Titanic.

20

THE SHIFTING GRAVES OF LOGIERAIT

F E BIRCH

If you were to go to the graves of Logierait, about six miles before Pitlochry, just off the A9 travelling north, you might be bemused to see the cast-iron cages and the black chains and locks. A tale for another time that harks back to Burke and Hare, the grave-robbers extraordinaire who ravaged the newly buried coffins for their wares. What you might not be prepared for, though, are the wailing evil fae creatures we know as the Unseelie Court. I've told my children and now warn my grandchildren, but will they listen? Naw, they all end up finding oot for themsels. This is my story from when I was a lass. Buckle in, for I can never forget...

When Shona said she had the number six, I knew it wasn't the local bus but a pack of cigarettes, ten of the best our money could buy. How could I refuse?

Nothing was more important than Sunday evenings at five o'clock and the top forty countdown with Radio One DJ Alan "Fluff" Freeman. It was as essential as breathing, and we waited all week for it back in 1975. Although I didn't fancy the idea of the cemetery, the pull and tug of the fly ciggies whilst waiting to hear if Queen or Abba would take the number one slot compelled me to the graveside monuments of the eighteenth-century bodies that once lived in Logierait and beyond. Nowhere could get a radio reception like the east wall near the final resting place of farmer Rodney MacDougall, 1864 – 1937.

It was five minutes to five when Shona called. We had to rush to make it on time. Light rain turned heavy as we ran along the lane in the dark. Pit-pat-pit-pat water drops fell from our heads. We scurried past Cuil an Daraich, the workhouse now turned bed-and-breakfast. Was Dougie home, listening, trying but failing to record the charts because of his poor reception? I'd had my eye on Dougie Stewart since his family took over the

B'n'B. I liked the way his hair flicked up at the back and the way he lolloped as he walked and always ignoring us girls as we drooled over him.

We reached the gate leading to steep steps down to the entrance of the kirkyard, the congregation long since gone, no mourners straggling by on this dreich Sunday teatime. Shona slid the latch and shouted, 'Hurry up, Eilidh.' I snagged my hair on a hawthorn bush that bore the remnants of berries, all shrivelled and dark red. Thorny branches stuck in my hair and scratched my face. I brushed them away and hurried to take refuge by the mossy knoll where Shona laid the plastic blanket, right next to old man MacDougall.

Days like this, I thanked her for being a Girl Guide. She remembered things like the blanket, a torch and most of all, the lighter.

'Get the fags oot,' I ordered, slumping down beside her, disentangling thorns from my hair.

'Dark, ainnit,' she said, a statement, not a question.

I shivered and tutted. 'We should find somewhere else but too late now. Grant ya though, it's a bit spooky.' I snuggled up to her shoulder, for comfort, for warmth, for friendship. 'Tha's nawhere. We've already tried. Get the tranny going, Eilidh. I'll light up if you tune up.'

I took oot the little transistor radio and pulled up the aerial notch by notch, almost poking myself in the eye. Crackle and hiss gave way to The Walker Brothers singing 'No Regrets'.

'Turn it up, Eils,' Shona demanded as she handed me a lit cigarette. She blew a huge puff of smoke, and a screech filled the darkness.

I squealed and dropped the cigarette onto my lap.

Shona laughed and fell to the side. 'It's only an owl.'

Owl or otherwise, I was truly spooked. I leant back against the damp wall and wet moss seeped into the back of my jacket.

'Yeah, well. It gave me a shock.' I took a deep drag of the fag and puckered up my lips to blow rings of smoke like an old Indian chief. I did four good ones. 'How many can you do, Shoan? More than five?' Donna Summer crooned 'love to love you baby'. The air around us filled with smoke as I reached for another cigarette. The rain eased off, but the temperature had dropped.

I looked around us and I realised it wasn't smoke but a chilly mist.

'I'm freezing, Shona. Don't suppose you have a camping stove in your bag?' I saw her looking toward the river. Her face wore strange features – not fear, nor curiosity, but a mix of the two and something else again I didn't recognise.

She raised a hand and pointed. 'What's that?'

'Stop trying to scare me. I don't know an owl from a banshee but—'

Another sorrowful screech rang oot. It hung suspended in the air and we both screamed, grabbing hold of each other in a jumble of arms, heads and legs.

'I don't think that was an owl,' said Shona.

My heart beat fast as adrenaline pumped through my body. I took a few deep breaths, tried to reason, to convince myself as well as her. 'We're being daft. We're spooked. It was an owl. There's nothing there.'

'But I saw it. A woman. In white. Maybe grey. Standing by the river. Swaying.'

'What, the Grey Lady?' I laughed without substance. It wasn't funny. 'No such thing as the Grey Lady. Pass me the lighter. And tune the radio.'

The music had disappeared and was replaced with static. Shona twiddled the knobs and twisted the aerial. I pulled my jacket down and shuffled back against the wall. The mist started to lift. 'Got any chocolate?' I asked.

Shona handed me the lighter and a pack of chewing gum. 'Naw, it was your turn to bring it.'

'I forgot.'

'You always do.' She messed on with the radio and 'Evil Woman' played oot. One of my favourites. New at number twenty-five. Twenty-five? We were on number thirty-two only a few minutes ago. 'What time is it?' I asked.

Shona looked at her watch. 'Quarter to six.'

Where did the last half hour go?

Shona tapped the glass face of her watch as ELO finished, and "Fluff" Freeman told us Hot Chocolate were at twenty-two with 'You Sexy Thing'. Smoky mist wound around us once more. 'Look! Over there!' hissed Shona, pointing in the direction of the river.

I saw it. I saw *her*, standing there, against the silhouette of the black trees that reached up into the starry night. She was a tall woman with silvery hair, the same colour as her face, same colour as her dress. She hovered by the bank then bent down. She was digging, searching for something. The radio hissed and wailing bounced around us, becoming louder, more sorrowful, mournful.

Shona stood up, eyes fastened on the woman. She took a step forward and I tugged on her duffel coat.

'Stay here,' I hissed.

She ignored me and pulled away from my grasp. She walked toward the river, weaving her way through the headstones toward the woman, avoiding fallen memorials and sunken pockets of earth as if on automatic, like she could clearly see the way in the deepest of the dark. I scrabbled up and followed her. 'Shona. Shona!'

As we both moved closer to the woman, me stumbling as I went, I saw she was washing something in the river – cloths, each the same colour as her dress. I could see that she wasn't much older than us. Twenty, maybe. Pretty and so very thin. And she looked so, so cold. She sang a lament, a song of death. I shivered as goosepimples sprang up on my head and down my neck.

Shona was a few paces ahead of me, near to the iron-caged graves that protected tombs of a man, woman, and child, that had been kept safe since the times of the grave-robbers who plundered all our kirkyards back in the day. We'd learned about them in school but tonight they were sinister and eerie and best avoided. Shona neared the river. She bent down and picked up a silver comb. The woman turned, stood and held oot both arms toward Shona, her dress shimmering white, grey and silver in the wet air. I wanted to scream, to stop Shona and run, but I couldn't move. I was stuck. I couldn't walk, couldn't talk. I was rooted to the spot and compelled to watch as Shona handed the comb to the woman, who gave a silvery smile. A screech filled the air, piercing my ears. I closed my eyes tight and held my hands to my head, trying to stop my ears from bursting.

Then it stopped.

I opened my eyes.

The mist had disappeared and so had Shona and the woman. I ran to the riverbank. 'Shona! Shona!' I was frantic. Where had she gone? Where had the woman taken her? The river, although not that wide, was running fast. It had been raining for the last three days and snow from the mountains had melted, causing the river to swell. She must be in the water.

'Shona! Shona!' I ran first to the right, then realised the river flowed the other way, so ran off to the left, searching in the dark, trying to find my friend. She might have become caught in roots or stuck between rocks. My stomach began churning, whirling. My chest was tight. Where was she? The torch! I had to find it. I turned and ran back to old MacDougall's grave. As I snatched up the torch I saw Dougie Stewart walking along the top pavement, head hunched down, fists punched into his coat pockets.

'Dougie? Dougie?'

He turned, grunted at me and kept walking.

I shouted louder. 'Please help, Dougie. It's Shona. She's gone missing. I think she's in the water!'

He stopped. 'What? You serious?'

'I wouldn't joke.'

He leapt down the stone steps. 'Why d'ya think she's in tha river, Eilidh?'

He knew my name. Fleeting hope flooded through me but I didn't have time to think about that now. I needed to find Shona.

'We were listening to the charts. There was a woman. By the river. Wailing. Shona went to her and now they're both gone. We have to find her. Please. I think she might have fallen in. It's flowing real fast.'

I heard Dougie mutter 'Banshee' but ignored it as I pulled on his arm to hurry him to the riverbank. I flicked on the torch which gave us feeble light. When we reached the protected graves, I told Dougie, 'This is where she picked up the comb.'

'She picked up a comb? A silver comb?'

'I think so. Why?' How did he know it was silver? Maybe he had a girlfriend and he'd brought her here and she'd lost a comb. Wouldn't that be just typical?

'The legend. The banshee calls and lays a trap for a mortal, usually a silver comb. Whoever picks it up is spirited away. Taken, gone.'

I laughed shakily. 'Rubbish!'

'Serious. It's written. Legend.'

'We have to find her.' I dragged him behind me, searching up and down the river, looking for some sign of Shona. We searched for ten minutes, fear setting in further, the more time passed.

'We're going to have to go for help,' I said. 'The river could have taken her halfway to Perth by now.' Tears I'd been fighting began to spill, falling hot down my cold face. I swept them away.

'There! What's that?' shouted Dougie from further up the riverbank.

I ran and shone the torch in the direction he was pointing. Dark material was caught in the willow branches that hung over the water. 'It looks like Shona's coat.'

Dougie scrambled to it but missed his step. He slipped down the muddy bank and his foot slid into the water. He yanked himself up and snatched the coat. As he pulled it, I saw it was Shona's duffel. 'No! No!' I sobbed. I clambered over to him but slipped, falling onto my back. The wet earth clogged in my hair. My feet hit the water, bitter cold. As I tried to pull back, my foot hit something soft. 'Dougie! Dougie!' He pulled me up and reached down into the water.

'It's Shona!'

We hauled my friend from the freezing river, her body so cold, so waterlogged. I thought she must be dead. I was convinced she was.

'She's still breathing, Eilidh. She's still alive.' Dougie's voice cracked, such a soft, lilting voice, so kind. My hero. But I didn't have time to think about him any further. Shona was unconscious and we needed to get help. We carried her between us, back through the cemetery, respecting the graves by walking around them, not over them, past the iron-clad tombs, and old MacDougall's headstone. As we weaved our way to the steps, the transistor radio suddenly blared oot Freddie Mercury singing about being caught in a landslide. 'Queen's still number one then,' Dougie said.

Two days later, I took the bus to Perth Royal Infirmary with a bag of grapes and a bottle of Lucozade. And chocolate. I didn't forget the chocolate.

We were lucky to find Shona when we did. She'd slipped, banged her head on one of the fallen headstones and fallen into the river. The water had carried her along and she'd become snagged in the low-hanging willow. Although unconscious, her head hadn't gone under water. A few more minutes and she might have.

Shona grabbed my hand. 'Eilidh, you won't believe what happened. Promise not to tell?'

'I'm saying nothing about smoking.'

'Not that. But yes, don't tell. Dad would kill me. When you found me I wasn't unconscious. I was with them... the faeries. You must have broken the magic, stepped over the boundary or something. You remember the woman?'

'The banshee woman? Yeah.'

'Well, she's in mourning, for the dead—'

'It's a kirkyard, Shona. There are plenty of dead people in there.'

'All those gravestones that are wonky? Those near the river-bank? When the river swells, the banks break. All those graves at the edge have sunk and the bodies, or rather their skeletons, they've shifted, moved oot into the fields on the other side and beyond.'

'How do you know that? What's it got to do with the banshee?'

'If you stop interrupting... The people, those skeletons, they're lost souls. They need to find their way back to their final resting place. The banshee is mourning them, calling them home, like a foghorn, like the one at St Andrew's, you know? The comb I picked up. That was a trap, to entice a mortal, a real person, to help to restore the souls.'

She was being weird, bizarre. 'Dougie told me about the comb being a trap...'

'He's right. It was. When she started wailing, really wailing, she grabbed my hand and swept me with her, and we went right under the river, and I met faeries. They're Seelie Courts. You heard of them?'

I shook my head, bewildered at her tale.

'They're good faeries, and they live in the air and underground. On the Sabbath they come oot and do good deeds. They were helping the banshee restore the lost souls back to their proper graves. They're beautiful, Eils, shimmering with gold and green and red colours. They're so pure. Beautiful creatures.' Her eyes brightened and I could see she was in another place. Then her face darkened.

'But some bad faeries came. The Unseelie Court. There was a huge battle. They're really evil and they dress in black, with kilts like tutus and horrid masks and vicious sgian-dubhs. They bleed, too, you know, the faeries. Bleed red, like us.' She paused. 'Whenever the riverbank collapses, the Unseelie Court pull bodies from the graves and push them oot to be carried along in the current, all across the Tay.'

'Shona. You had a bang on the head. You haven't said anything to the doctors, have you? Because I don't think that would be a good thing. You'll end up in Murray Royal, the mental hospital.'

'I'm telling the truth. The faeries, they're real.'

I muttered, 'Away with the faeries, more like.'

'You don't believe me.' Her eyes shone and she turned her head away.

I took her hand and squeezed it. 'Just what was in those cigarettes, my friend?'

'I know you think I'm silly, but it was real. The nurse told me the kirkyard is haunted and those graves, they're called the Shifting Graves of Logierait.'

I sighed. 'I do believe you. Dougie told me the legend yesterday, when he came over.'

She smiled. 'Oh! So, he's your boyfriend now?'

'Well… he did ask me oot.' I shrugged, all shy.

'Oh good! I asked the Seelie Court if they could make a wish come true. And they have. I'm so happy for you.' She squeezed my hand. 'And I think 'Mamma Mia' might just be number one this week.' She held up her other hand, fingers crossed.

'No more kirkyards though,' I said. 'Dougie gets a great reception at the back of his house and his mum's invited us both over this Sunday, if you're up for it. He's a local hero now, you know.'

'Aye. No more kirkyards. Pinkie swear!'

We hooked little fingers. Friends for life. Faeries not included…

AS WE HOLD the service for my Dougie this week, I've made sure he's being cremated. No Shifting Graves of Logierait for us. Our grandchildren will carry his coffin, and we will remember them, the faeries good and bad, for we've seen them often since that night in 1975.

21

THE WHITE WIDOW

GAVIN BOYTER

I'm almost certainly the postman at the highest altitude in the British Isles, not a claim to fame I ever envisaged in my youth. Assynt's rocky trails, many of them eroded into a slurry of mud and gravel by autumn storms, are treacherous at the best of times, and the stretch I'm currently walking, between Culnacraig and Dun Canna, is especially forbidding.

The fact that it's snowing heavily, and has been for several hours, should have given me pause. The woman who owns the guest house, at which I am the only resident, accosted me only this morning, armed with a pot of tea, scones, a sad shake of the head and the words, 'Ah well, you'll no be wand'ring the postie's path the mornin'.'

She said it as if it were a foregone conclusion, but I am adamantine when I've a scheme in mind and today would be no different. And so, belly filled at seven with a hearty cooked breakfast, then a second, entirely gratuitous second breakfast, I set off, with my Swiss walking poles, Arctic cagoule, woollen hat, heavy gloves, two pairs of socks and sensibly cleated footwear. I may be a little reckless, but I'm not entirely stupid.

My current mission began, as many such missions do, when I became irreparably lost on an obscure trail, one leading from the site of the prehistoric fort at Dun Canna north-east to the village of Strathcanaird. This occurred a month ago on the last trip I took with my wife Emily before she finally succumbed to that degenerate little tumour in her frontal lobe.

Emily sat by the fire in a local pub, reading, while I set out on what was to be my last trail run. I'd just turned seventy-two and my knees weren't up to the task of louping up rockfaces or shuddering down scree slopes. It had become too dangerous. Besides, even walking these remote Scottish outposts in one's fading decades is an act of exceptional optimism. The weather changes with fearful suddenness and fair becomes foul at the whim of the gods.

I'd made it four miles in, following the course of a burn. I was smugly glad I'd thought to wear plastic bags over my socks before putting on my hiking boots, a trick of my own invention. The boots were sodden from waterlogged stretches of peaty moorland, but my feet remained cosy. However, the rain progressed gradually from a misty smirr to a diagonal deluge. After an hour of this, having utterly lost the sheep path I'd been following, I began to have recurring fantasies of joining my wife in the Twa Corbies pub, whisky at hand, crackling fire warming my extremities. In that moment, my willpower broke, and I turned for home, immediately tripped over a rock and fell face-first into the heather.

The stumble didn't hurt or injure me, and nor was my pride much affected – I abandoned that luxury when old age began to render it redundant. Besides, there was nobody bar a few bedraggled sheep to notice my fall.

I turned to see what I'd tripped over, and there, half concealed by bracken, was a hewn stone, rather like a miniature headstone, or mile marker, its base firmly implanted in the soil. I pushed wet fronds aside to examine it. It was a piece of lichen-speckled granite, but it appeared to have indentations carved into one side. I looked closer and fancied I could make out the shape of a feminine face in profile, and a border of decorative swirls. It was a familiar shape but one that escaped my understanding until I made it back to the pub and recounted the incident to my wife.

'Ha!' she simply laughed once I'd finished my narrative. 'Then you fared better than the last man who stumbled there.'

What on earth was she talking about? I asked her to explain her cryptic utterance and she unfolded a strange story that made sense of my wayward wanderings. She'd abandoned her novel for one of the books from the Corbies' own miniature library, mostly folklore, mawkish poetry, and local history. One of these texts was entitled *Postal Paths and Drove Roads of Assynt* by Herbert B Mannheim. The maps in the middle of this text had piqued her interest.

'It seems that once the penny post was initiated,' Emily explained, 'the local postal service received a flood of business. People began sending one another postcards, small gifts, love letters and other communications previously considered excessive. This created a problem of volume and efficiency for the postal office, which had to send a horse and carriage along old military roads and overgrown drove paths. They decided to enlist a team of fit young men to shoulder backpacks full of correspondence and walk them over the more direct, but treacherous footpaths. They did this so efficiently, they'd sometimes beat carriages forced to take much longer routes.

'Of course, quite frequently there would be accidents, and even deaths,' Emily explained, her tone darkening. One such mishap befell a nineteen-year-old youth recruited to the postal service from Glasgow. He'd been teased by some of the local boys. They'd mentioned a grim spectre – a young, veiled woman who'd lead men astray. Although it was almost certainly an attempt to terrify this new recruit, one Hamish McAlpine, for cruel satisfaction, there was a link to local folklore, Emily revealed. Songs and poems told of a "white widow" who'd walk the hills and crags, and could transform into a seagull, a skirl of mist or even a sheet of windblown snow.

'She was widowed on the eve of her wedding, they say,' Emily explained, 'and hanged herself wearing her wedding dress. Folks think she wanders these lands searching for the shade of her fiancé, a farmer who'd perished in a terrible snowstorm.'

'So, they scared this young postman with the story,' I said. 'What has that to do with my falling over in the heather?'

'The headstone,' Emily said. 'Some think it's there to honour the farmer who died, since it's right in the middle of his family's grazing land. The woman depicted is supposed to be his betrothed. But others say it's dedicated to Hamish McAlpine. You see, he never returned from his first foray out on the postal paths. His body was never found.'

'But the carving on the stone...' I said, and here Emily seemed to anticipate me, as she often did.

'It's a Penny Black.'

Of course. That's why the image was so familiar – the young Victoria, ornately framed. My grandfather's philately books I'd pored over as a child.

'You're amazing,' I said, bending to kiss my wife on the forehead. There was an odd clamminess about her skin, despite her proximity to the fire. I should have sensed she'd be taken from me within weeks. We didn't spend nearly enough time together on that last trip, a regret I suspect will never leave me.

Emily had mentioned that there was a small collection of local antiquities in the village hall, so I waited out that wet weekend, and then, at 10am on Monday morning, we took a stroll to the small but sturdy stone building which contained a little meeting room, a low, curtained stage, and a couple of side rooms. One of these had a handwritten sign on its door, reading *Local Collections*. The young woman who staffed the reception desk, Miss Finian, unlocked this door for us and led us through to a musty, damp-smelling library with a writing desk, a few church pews, a plan chest and three bookcases. Two of these were filled with old tomes too tedious to relate. The middle case, however, was a glass-fronted display of miscellaneous artifacts including Pictish jewellery, pieces of a Viking helmet and, oddest of all, an envelope, bearing the remnants of a blob of sealing wax, but no stamp or postmark. The card beneath this last item read, *Letter, found on the high path by Dun Canna, thought undelivered.*

'Could that have belonged to Hamish McAlpine?' I couldn't help but wonder aloud.

'That it could!' came a stout voice from behind us, making me start. We turned and saw a reddish-faced man in his late forties standing there, rocking on his heels. He thrust out a meaty paw, which, after some hesitation, I shook.

'Geoff Truss,' he said, as if his name explained something. 'Local postman, and general busybody.'

Over Truss's shoulder I saw Miss Finian raise an arch eyebrow as she hovered solicitously.

'Are you the writers?' He beamed. I'd forgotten how fast word travels in such tiny communities.

'Well, *I'm* a writer. My wife's an academic.'

Emily tutted. 'And a writer too,' she admonished, brushing her hand against Truss's. 'Though only if sixteenth-century Italian poetry is your cup of tea.'

Then she laughed in that generous, mellifluous way that never failed to melt my heart. Emily made everyone feel welcome and included. Moments later, she and Truss were fast friends, and we were sitting huddled on a pew like co-conspirators, discussing the history of the postal paths which Truss, unsurprisingly, knew rather a lot about.

There, in that drafty village hall, and later, in the firelit lounge of the Corbies, a strange plan developed. A scheme that I shared only with Emily. One I'm now enacting, here on this storm-scoured cliff face.

The idea was so exciting that I called my editor immediately, pitching a semi autobiographical account of wandering the postal paths of Assynt, carrying the last, undelivered letter of a young, tragically slain postman. Exactly the kind of thing the glossy supplement in question laps up. I had my commission within minutes. I was so carried away by both my own and my editor's enthusiasm that I entirely forgot to answer one vital question. How would I get hold of the letter?

Fortunately, once again, Emily solved my conundrum.

'Tell them you've arranged to have it DNA tested at my university, so they can know once and for all if it was handled by Hamish McAlpine. They've got bits of his uniform. It'll certainly have hairs or skin flakes. My colleagues in the genetics lab can run a quick check.'

'Will they do that?'

'They will if I sweet-talk them. In the meantime, you can take it on your weird little pilgrimage, if it means so much to you.'

I couldn't really explain it to her, but somehow it did. Emily fired off an email to a friend at the university, although we had to leave for Edinburgh before we got a reply. Before that happened, however, Emily's condition abruptly worsened, and she was hospitalised. She died just six days later.

After the funeral, and all the rigmarole around her will and last wishes, I let my routine slide rather, until my son Gareth prompted me to shake myself out of my funk. I finally felt able to read my emails a week ago. I found three of immediate interest among the condolences, offers of assistance, and junk mail.

The first was from Emily's colleague's laboratory, confirming the booking for the document DNA check. The second was a gentle prompt from the magazine editor who wanted my Assynt piece. The third, however, was the clincher. It was from Emily.

She must have sent it a couple of days before she passed. I've no idea how, since I was at her bedside constantly, yet somehow my wife managed to cajole me from beyond the grave.

After relaying many fond reminiscences too painful to relate here, the message ended with a curt command: *Do not mope!* Then a single kiss and her familiar, ornate e-signature.

And that's why I'm here, tottering along this snow-blasted edge, where the contour lines seem to stumble over one another, and my feet are liable to do likewise. I'm a ridiculous old man, pursuing this perilous quest, and I'm probably going to end up the same way as the White Widow's fiancé and Hamish the novice postie, perishing here on a frozen nub overlooking the Atlantic.

I've lost the proper path to Culnacraig, and the slim runnel I'm following now is spotted with suspiciously large numbers of sheep droppings. The path veers away from the sheer edge of the cliffs, below which seabirds whirl, and heads uphill and inland, alongside a row of tormented trees. Too gnarly to identify, they resemble beseeching penitents, their hands stretched out toward a thin, V-shaped valley through which a burn tumbles. I make for it, noting that a similar blue vein is marked upon my map.

In my backpack there's a Ziploc bag containing the letter found near Dun Canna. Emily, Miss Finian, Truss and I examined it with a magnifying glass before I carefully placed it between sheets of plastic and PVC. The name and address, oddly enough, were just visible, although the writing on the letter itself seems to have faded into insubstantiality.

'Perhaps written with a different pen, and less durable ink?' Miss Finian opined. Of course, we had no way of knowing if the single sheet of paper folded into quarters within the onion-skin-thin envelope had ever contained writing. Perhaps some odd character had mailed a love token, such as a pressed flower, or a lock of hair, concealed within that vellum sheet, a sentimental trifle now lost to the ages.

What we did know was that the letter was addressed as follows:

The Lady in the Last House, by the Falls at Balwhinnie.

And that was all.

'Must be the row of abandoned crofts,' Truss muttered. 'There's bugger all of consequence there now.'

I couldn't help but wonder though. Was this letter addressed to the White Widow herself? Was it part of some elaborate prank by the postie's colleagues? On later examination, however, the timeline didn't work. Six months passed between the death of the betrothed crofters and young McAlpine setting out on his fateful journey. Whatever this message said would remain mysterious. I liked not knowing, I convinced myself – it would give me more to speculate about in my essay.

That is, if I ever reach my destination. The snow, which had consisted of thin, confetti-like swirls, is now coming down in concentrated sheets, slicing across my path and eroding the very sheep track I'm walking. There's an eerie silence to it – like a television channel detuned to static, with the sound turned down. I feel winter's fingers penetrating my many layers, burrowing into the gap between scarf and coat, clasping at my ankles whenever my trouser leg rides up. Still, I press on.

I could hardly do otherwise. I estimate I've been walking for two and a half hours and am just five miles into my walk, with two more to go. I look at my wristwatch, a gift from Emily, allowing icy flakes to caress my wrist for a moment. 2.55pm. At this time of year, it will be dark by four. I'd better hurry.

I begin to march, stiff-legged, chin pushed down onto my chest. This continues for agonising, incalculable minutes. I hear a waterfall's tumult pierce the fearful silence. I look up and the path has vanished, although the valley's dark slash can still just be discerned through the whiteout. Then something altogether stranger occurs.

The descending flakes seem to spiral together before me, perhaps simply in an eddying current of air. And yet for a fanciful moment, they seem to form a shape – a feminine form, arm outstretched, pointing... I rub my eyes, certain I'm delirious. I can't have seen a figure swathed in white, head shawled in some sort of... veil. This is perhaps the first indication of a dangerous chill. Can people experiencing the first signs of hypothermia hallucinate?

When I open my watery eyes, most of the form has vanished yet a head, shoulder and arm still float for a split-second, before dissolving on the wind. I follow the line of the spectre's finger. I spy the merest suggestion of a path, a deeper channel of fresh snow among the hummocky heather and march on, trying not to dwell upon what I've seen. Suggestion can be a remarkable thing, and I've been thinking of little more than the White Widow, and my Emily for the last several hours.

I follow the possible path toward the waterfall's roar and there it is – half frozen into icicles, concealed and then revealed between granite slabs of shattered mountainside. My boots slip and slither, as I clamber among the wet rocks. There, I finally spot what I've been looking out for – the remains of a cut stone, long and oblong and spotted with moss, but undeniably a lintel.

Around it, there are several piles of old stones, and fragments of long-rotten wood, indicating that a house once stood here, with its back to the falls and its face to the sea. Between cascade and ocean's roar, and certainly the last croft at Balwhinnie.

I duck behind a long, slanting slab which offers some respite from the blizzard. Shucking off my pack, I open it, unzip the document folder with shaking hands, and extract the clear Ziploc bag. I'm not sure what I expect to happen, but I have an unaccountable craving to press the ancient letter against the lintel stone. I should not unzip the bag and take the paper out, I think, while finding myself doing exactly that.

A flash of the White Widow's spectral head, slowly turning to face me, flickers into mind and I panic, picking at the paper as the wind catches it and whirls it out of my grasp.

'No!' I shout, thinking of the trouble I'll provoke if I lose this precious local artifact. I run from my enclosure, leaping into deep snow and clutching for the spinning, teasing parchment. And of course, I fall there, tumbling helplessly as so many have before me. The farmer, McAlpine the postie, and now Benjamin Tulloch – writer, widower, hillwalker, and miscreant. I fall, and blackness comes rushing in, with the blizzard its veiled companion.

Two things stand out from the dream that soon pursues me. First, the unaccountable fragrance of mountain thyme, and secondly, a fragment of an old song, one I'd read with Emily, by the freshly stoked fire of the Twa Corbies Inn.

I will twin thee a bow'r
By the clear silver fountain,
And I'll cover it o'er
Wi' the flooers o' the mountain.
I will range through the wilds
And the deep glens sae dreary,
And return wi' their spoils
Tae the bow'r o' my dearie.

Will ye go, lassie, go, I add, feeling an unaccountable warmth on both eyelids – a delicate kiss, such as Emily once bestowed.

I spasm back into consciousness, opening my eyes to see a sky darkening but thankfully free from icy petals spiralling down. I have no idea how long I'd lain there, perhaps a couple of minutes, maybe more, before something woke me. I don't discover this until much later that day, but there's a small gash in my scalp. It's just under the hairline, and the blood has frozen stiff within my matted locks. My face and extremities feel oddly warm. I know this can't be a good thing, so I haul myself stiffly to my feet and look about me.

There is my backpack, half covered in snow in the lee of the granite slab. And there, remarkably, just six feet away, is the letter, wet through and wrapped like a lover's embrace around the lintel stone. I very gently peel it free and slip it back into the Ziploc bag. My watch reveals that I have only blacked out momentarily. That said, every minute counts on an Assynt winter's evening, so I grit my teeth, sling the backpack over my shoulder and begin to power up the rocky path I can now clearly discern crossing the top of the waterfall and continuing up and over the ridge.

A little under forty minutes later I reach Culnacraig, where a very worried Geoff Truss is waiting in his red Post Office van, having arranged to meet me there and drive me back to my guest house. I'd only told him about my plan to walk the postal routes alone; I'd shared nothing about the presence of the letter in my backpack.

'What kept you?' he jokes, relief flooding his features as he ushers me into the warm vehicle.

'Waylaid by the White Widow,' I reply as deadpan as I can muster, while wondering if what I've just jokingly suggested is literally true. If I have encountered a phantasm, was she pointing to her long-destroyed domicile, or to the path to safety? Were her motives self-serving or charitable?

Three days later I'm back in Edinburgh and heading to a potentially futile rendezvous. I've carefully dried off the nineteenth-century missive, in a takeaway box layered with muslin on top of a radiator turned down low. I'm now due to hand it over to Professor Sarah Hamlyn of the Historic Documents Department at Edinburgh University.

'What are you hoping to find out?' the surprisingly young yet sincere professor asks me, almost as if I'm handing over a long-cherished family heirloom.

I sigh. 'Oh, anything at all. Here's a couple of hairs from the postman who may have attempted to deliver the letter.'

I hand over the tiny test tube that Miss Finian gave me, containing two tiny, twisted fibres which she assured me came from Hamish McAlpine's bunnet.

'Don't hope for too much,' Professor Hamlyn cautions. 'After this length of time, the chances of getting any live DNA are slim.'

So it proves. I know from the regretful cast of the Professor's head when I meet her in her departmental offices ten days later, that she's found nothing definitive.

'We can't say for certain who handled the letter and in fact, we couldn't even find evidence that anything had been written on it.'

I nod, expecting as much. A disappointing end to a long-overdue article. My editor will not be pleased.

'Well, there was one odd thing,' she adds, almost in consolation. 'We detected the presence of some sort of herb, perhaps thyme? I might even speculate...'

Here Professor Hamlyn pauses, leaning in like a naughty schoolgirl.

'Well, it's possible that a love token, such as a sprig of mountain thyme, was enclosed. It was often a component of wedding favours, worn close to the bride's breast. Would that make any sense?'

I have an extraordinary and instant realisation. I'm certain of it.

The letter had nothing to do with my wayward postman at all. McAlpine might simply have found the letter on his wanderings that day, and felt compelled to deliver it, even months after the doomed farmer had addressed it. This would explain the absence of a stamp. I had completed McAlpine's kind-hearted but foolish last delivery, and the White Widow had blessed me for it.

'It makes perfect sense, Professor,' I reply, without elaborating. I somehow don't want to share my theory. It feels too... intimate.

Professor Hamlyn frowns slightly, the two tiny furrows on either side of her nose at the brow reminding me of Emily's quizzical expression when humouring me.

I suppose I will always be pursuing my ghosts, whether wandering snow-scattered moorlands or simply dreaming. After all, we are all walking fading trails with only one ultimate destination.

ABOUT THE AUTHORS

Jeannette Ellwood: Jeannette spent her career in education, fostering independent thought and a spirit of adventure. She has travelled widely, published a book about her journeys, *Nuns, Guns & Disappearing Suns* (with Sue Mowforth) and is currently writing a memoir about life in wartime London. A lifelong lover of animals – from childhood snails to Arab horses – she draws inspiration from memory, landscape and the natural world.

Chauntelle Wright: A Lancashire-based writer and charity professional whose non-fiction on money and debt has appeared in industry journals since 2008. Now returning to her childhood love of storytelling, she is completing a book-club-worthy historical crime novel exploring justice, a theme close to her heart. This short story marks her fiction debut.

Campbell Christie: I've dreamt of being a published writer since I was old enough to write, and storytelling has always been at the heart of who I am. I hold a BA (Hons) in Print Media and went on to study Copywriting and Screenwriting. Along the way, my feature script *Lunar Jetman* became a finalist in the 2020 Austin Film Festival, and I've had short stories published in online magazines.

With Scottish heritage inspiring much of my work, I love exploring folklore and reimagining it in fresh ways, while also writing across multiple genres to keep challenging myself. *The Wulver* is my debut novel, a folklore inspired werewolf retelling, which I'm excited to be self-publishing.

TH Wilson: From the north-east of England. When not writing she can be found walking her rescue greyhound, camping with her husband or spending time with family. She enjoys crafting and finds it therapeutic, this also helps with ideas for stories, letting her mind wander and plot as she goes.

Nico: A multifaceted writer with over three decades of creative expression, Nico has built a dynamic career as a writer, filmmaker and advertising executive – anchored by a deep command of storytelling. A published author with several original works, he focuses on narratives that explore universal themes of love, isolation, guilt, the unravelling mind and the fragility of life. His work draws on diverse literary influences – Roald Dahl, Charles Dickens and Patricia Highsmith – crafted to resonate across cultures and generations.

Sue Mowforth: Sue is a superb storyteller. Although many of her tales sound incredible, many are, in fact, true for she has led an adventurous life. She has lived and worked in various parts of the world and has been an air traffic controller, pilot, teacher, mother, traveller and writer. You will find some of her tales in *Nuns, Guns & Disappearing Suns*, co-authored with Jeannette Ellwood and available on Amazon.

Peter Crickmore: Peter has nearly always been a writer, but his turn with fiction came late in life.

A graduate engineer, his first jobs were technical and business articles for McGraw Hill and for other magazines when they were the prime source of business intelligence. He progressed naturally into editing and publishing, *inter alia*, and joining United Nations missions in Vienna and Kosovo. His writing work also enabled long stays in the United States and the Far East.

He is currently working on a fantasy novel wherein the plant world moves against humans to save the planet from environmental catastrophe.

Les Wood: I've had numerous short stories and poems published in various anthologies, and I have previously been a winner of the Canongate Prize for New Writing and a prize-winner in the McCash Scots Poetry competition. My novel, *Dark Side of the Moon* was published in late 2016 by Freight Books and was listed by Booklist as one of the top ten crime novels of 2017. I have had invited appearances at the Bloody Scotland crime-writing festival and the AyeWrite! Glasgow book festival. My second novel, *Close to the Edge* is currently wandering the wilds looking for a publisher.

Jane Morgan: Having co-authored a volume called *Nicknames: Their Origins and Social Consequences* in 1979, Jane Morgan has had a forty-year break from publishing. As a lecturer, her decades long involvement, commitment and many roles in the Access and A Level programmes in Milton Keynes College ensured her working life was "never boring". Retirement has meant she can indulge her other interests, so she has since managed to visit every continent; tried her hand at watercolours and enjoyed relearning mah-jong and Welsh. She tries to start each day with some yoga and, far more difficult, to rise to the monthly challenges presented by the Towcester u3a Writing group.

. . .

Jack Wright: Jack is a horror writer from Blackburn, Lancashire, where he lives with his wife and three children. His fiction leans into the atmospheric and uncanny, with his debut novel, *Duskfield Pines*, set for release in 2026, followed by *Anna's Veil*.

David J Aitken is a writer from Scotland. A member of Glasgow's Thi Wurd writers group, being part of a community of writers both inspires his work and is a source of great learning, helping to deepen his understanding of the craft. Having written two unpublished novels, and currently working on a third, he rather hopes his next big project might just be the one. If not, he's got plenty ideas for a fourth and a fifth and probably even a sixth. Writing for the joy of it, he's happiest in front of the blank page, and happier still when the story begins to flow and the word count creeps slowly upward. He can be found on Twitter: @DavidJAitken and on Bluesky: @davidaitken.bsky.social.

Ewan Kirkwood: After years of loving reading and writing, I studied and graduated with an English Literature degree. This is my first piece of published material and I'm very grateful to Ian for taking this chance on me. I do not usually write supernatural fiction – crime/detective fiction is my forte. I am currently querying my first crime novel with agents and publishers.

Robin Barker: I'm from Cheltenham and I've been writing since I was young. It started out with short stories where I have won several competitions. I'm now editing/rewriting my horror novel.

I love writing, talking about writing and connecting with

other authors. You can find me on Instagram and Twitter: @robinbarker1 where I post pictures (not just of my cats), chat with my fellow writers and repost their successes.

CHRIS JAMES: I was born in Blandford, Dorset, and mostly grew up in Poole. After earning a degree in biology, I moved to London, where I worked as a medical scientist and later became a further education lecturer. Through a series of unexpected events, I found myself in education for the cleaning industry and then the waste management industry. One of my major achievements was serving as the technical author for the cleaning skills competition at EuroSkills, where the UK team won four gold medals. I am married, have four children, and live in a peaceful village in Northamptonshire. I primarily create stories with bizarre or comedic themes. My favourite authors include Jeff Wheeler, Bill Bryson, Bernard Cornwell, and J. R. R. Tolkien.

MICHAEL HAYES: I worked at the British Museum for many years but for health reasons took early retirement in 2020, whereupon I concentrated on my writing. I have recently completed an adult-themed book that features romance and murder for which I am now seeking a publisher.

I have written a series of short stories for the YA market, two of which have been published privately (Londoniarum Press). I have had articles published in various magazines and journals, including *The Lady* and *The British Museum Magazine.*

SUZIE WILDE: Suzie grew up between a cemetery and the Gravediggers Arms. Her Welsh mother could smell impending death and ghostly experiences were so normal that they never discussed them.

After success with magazine fiction and non-fiction, Suzie gained an MA with Distinction in Creative Writing and went on to write an epic Norse fantasy: *The Book of Bera*. The first of the trilogy was published in 2017 and the last of the series in 2023.

Her popular podcast Talking Books, with independent bookseller Tim O'Kelly, has lots of book suggestions and guest author interviews.

Links to all on her website: https://www.suziewilde.co.uk.

SARAH BURCHETT-COOK: I am an ex-academic with two non-fiction books published as a co-author. Fantasy has been my passion as a reader since I was a youngster, and now I'm equally passionate about the genre as a writer – and I'm on a mission to rediscover my magic!

I live in Scotland with my husband and find its otherworldly landscape and history a constant inspiration when I write. The novels, novellas and short stories I've written are often partially set here in Scotland. I'm fascinated by the idea of parallel worlds, and go out of my way to derive ways of bringing them to life. My website is: www.sarahburchettcook.co.uk.

MICHAEL THAME: Michael has written several ghost stories and edited three ghost story anthologies (*In Evil Memory*, *In a Darkened Room* and *Winter Marches On*). He is also the author of the Conyers Street Gang series of children's novels based on his grandparents' experiences during World War Two, which he reads to today's primary-school pupils dressed up as a 1920's Liverpool docker.

A former semi-professional rugby player, his day job is to be the founder and editor of *ScienceVega.com*, a website and quarterly online publication showcasing "Today's science to tomorrow's scientists" which is distributed free to GCSE+ science pupils. He was born in the Garden of England half a century ago and currently lives in Didsbury, south Manchester, with the author Jo Price (his non-wife – Covid cancelled the wedding) and dogs Daisy and Dexter. Finally, and most proudly, he is Dad to two wonderful daughters: Evie and Lily.

JOSS MOWFORTH: Joss is a British Army officer from Milngavie, just north of Glasgow. Raised in an old house steeped in history, he has long been drawn to eerie landscapes and unsolved mysteries. *Echoes from the Flannan Isles* was originally a short story he wrote at school for an English assignment, which he has subsequently rewritten to improve the childish language. It is his first published short story. When not writing, he enjoys hillwalking, historical research, and inventing increasingly daft endurance challenges (look up his name with the word "fridge" and you'll understand).

F E BIRCH is an ex-cop from the north-east of England. She is a short story and crime novel writer with a trail of pseudonyms and publications behind her. She won the first Bloody Scotland Pitch Perfect competition in 2012 with the premise of her debut novel, *She's Not There*. She wears many hats and her friends call her Effie. With a penchant for the dark, deep and disturbing, her crime stories are rarely cosy. Her books are listed on Amazon via various publishers and she can be found on most social media platforms as Effie Merryl. Her website is https://febirch.co.uk/.

. . .

Gavin Boyter: A Scottish writer and filmmaker living in Margate, Kent. He has published two travel memoirs about running ludicrously long distances, *Downhill from Here* and *Running the Orient*. The latter book charts his 2,300 mile run from Paris to Istanbul, following the 1883 route of the Orient Express. Gavin's stories have been published in *Constellations, DIAGRAM, Riptide, The Closed Eye Open, Ab Terra, Draw Down the Moon, La Piccioletta Barca* and *Freshwater Review*. He is also the writer-director of the 2015 independent film *Sparks & Embers*. In 2023 he published his debut novel *Elena in Exile*.

He can be found on TikTok: @margatewriter and Instagram: @gavin.boyter.

ABOUT THE EDITOR

Ian Skewis was offered the post of editor on a local freepaper in 1989 when he was aged nineteen. He turned it down in order to pursue a career in acting where he worked for the BBC and the Citizens' Theatre amongst others and which culminated in him playing the lead role in a stage play called *Like Thunder* which won the Edinburgh Fringe First Award in 2001. In 2017 he wrote his debut novel *A Murder Of Crows* which became a bestseller on Amazon and he narrated the audiobook which also became a bestseller. In 2019, aged forty-nine, he was offered the post of editor with a publishing house, Bloodhound Books. He accepted and has since edited over three hundred books (fiction and non-fiction) for authors and publishers. It's a funny old life...

Ian Skewis can be contacted via www.ianskewis.com.

ABOUT BRAE BOOKS

Brae Books was created by editor, author (and now publisher) Ian Skewis purely as a basis for the publication of this anthology. However, more books are in the pipeline. For those who are interested, the name Brae Books derives from the village of Hobbs Brae that was featured in Ian Skewis's bestselling debut novel *A Murder Of Crows*. Since then, Ian has moved to an area on the outskirts of Glasgow called Cathkin Braes. The name seems to have followed him and so here we are.

WWW.BRAEBOOKS.COM

Printed in Dunstable, United Kingdom

73828664R00138